PUSH-PUSH!

Sindiwe Magona

PUSH-PUSH!

and other stories

BEACON PRESS   *Boston*

Beacon Press
25 Beacon Street
Boston, Massachusetts 02108-2892
www.beacon.org

Beacon Press books
are published under the auspices of
the Unitarian Universalist Association of Congregations.

First Beacon Press edition published in 2001

Printed in the United States of America

05 04 03 02 01   7 6 5 4 3 2 1

This book is printed on acid-free paper that meets the
uncoated paper ANSI/NISO specifications for permanence
as revised in 1992.

Library of Congress Cataloging-in-Publication Data
Magona, Sindiwe.
    Push-push! and other stories / Sindiwe Magona.—1st Beacon
    Press ed.
        p. cm.—(Bluestreak)
    Contents: A drowning in Cala—House-hunting unlike
Soweto—Push-push!—Comrade, heal yourself!—I'm not talk-
ing about that, now—A peaceful exit—The widow—The hand
that kills—The sacrificial lamb—Bhelekazi's father.
    ISBN 0-8070-0967-9 (pbk.)
    1. South Africa—Social life and customs—Fiction. I. Title:
Half title: Push-push! II. Title. III. Series.

PR9369.3.M335 P87 2001
823'.914—dc21
                                              2001025731

With much love and grateful thanks to my
father-in-law, the Rev. Wilberforce Tukela Gobodo,
whose storytelling inspired this book

Contents

A Drowning in Cala

'There has been an accident!' The boy's voice, coming out in puffs, was hoarse. Absentmindedly, he kept rubbing his hands together, as if he were washing them.

'An accident?' 'Where?'

The two voices, screaming as one, pulled his thoughts back to the now; to the here.

But before he could give an answer, one of the men, Sandile, cried out: 'Would you all get out of the house! This boy of Mbhele's, Jonguhlanga, says there has been an accident!'

Turning to the boy, 'Who is hurt? How can we help? Where ...?' He screamed, not knowing that he did.

'We were bathing down by the river. And, and ...' The youth, fast approaching manhood, could not go on. He was a lanky lad for whom this summer was probably his last before circumcision, from which he would emerge a man. Hatless, he was barefoot and his pants sported patches here and there but were even so still torn and bare in parts. As *ikrwala*, all his clothes would be brand new, letting the whole world know of his metamorphosis. But as of now, no parent would waste money buying clothes for a boy that age; someone whom custom would forbid to wear any of those clothes after he was circumcised.

Hearing the commotion, several men, women, and children poured out of the five *rondavels* that made up the homestead and joined the men Jonguhlanga had found sitting on goat-skin mats near the cattle *kraal*. Even they were no longer sitting now, the news the boy had brought had catapulted them to their feet. Even Old Man Zengele, Sandile's father, forgot his arthritic knees and jumped up yelling:

'*Thetha, kwedini!* – Speak up, boy!' – before resting his elbow on a *knobkierrie* that, for the past year, had become his third leg. Then, noticing the women and children, he shouted:

'Is your work not waiting for you? Did anyone call your names, asking you to come to the men's *kraal*? Hunh?' More than words, however, the glint in the cold, narrowed eyes pitched the children and their mothers back inside.

The old man waited till the women were all inside, out of earshot. The children too. Then he turned his face back to the boy and urged:

'Now, tell us!'

Still the boy hesitated. He stammered.

'Don't be a woman,' scoffed the old man, hiding his anxiety in gruffy off-handedness.

'He ... he ... went down the water and didn't come back up. We ... He ... We ...'

He couldn't bring himself to say the name. Not looking at the man who was called by that name: *Tata kaZama*, Zama's father. His glazed and fear-filled eyes wandered onto the large frame of Sandile. Surely, something inside that big body must tell him it is his son I am here about? He heard his heart thudding as though he'd just finished running a very long mile, chased by a madman on horseback, a long, thick *sjambok* in his hand.

'*Kwedini!* Have you lost your tongue?' barked Zengele. He raised the walking-stick high up in the air and took a few tottering steps towards Jonguhlanga.

'Who did not come up?' Sandile heard himself ask; deep in his stomach a whole nest of voracious, tiny, tiny worms writhed.

Sandile and two other men left with the boy. Down to the river they ran, their hearts faster than their feet.

Left behind, Zengele lamented his crippled limbs that rendered him less useful than a babe in arms. 'What use old age,' he fumed aloud, addressing no one in particular, 'when the wisdom garnered with the passing of the years is of no count; encased in so brittle and feeble a vessel?' Just like one of the women, he thought, forced to wait on those who had gone to see with their own eyes the abomination Mbhele's son had come to report. Well, the old man consoled himself, the wait can't be that long; the shadows lengthen already. He shrugged his shoulders and went into his hut. There must be something there he could do. Deep at the back of his throat, sat a big, fat snake; coiled, the colour of venom.

He'd heard the fluttering wings of the bird of fear in the voice of his son. His son, fearing for his own. 'Who did not come up?' Sandile had asked. As though Mbhele's boy were an imbecile, who would run all the way up a steep hill to announce a calamity at the home of people to whom that was but an item of idle, local gossip.

When Sandile and his little group got to the river, they found a growing crowd already gathered. A young man detached himself from the assembly and came forward to meet them.

He led them a little downstream.

'This is where he went down,' he said, indicating a small cove.

And all could see how shallow the river was at that place. This would be a matter of much discussion later on. And many in the village would fail to see how a boy that age, all but a full-grown man, could drown in that part of the river. This is a river this child has swum since he was knee high, they said; he knows it left and right. Others would point to the season and wonder how anyone, let alone one conversant with the River Tsomo, could drown before the big rains of summer had come, 'drown at a time the river was almost dry'. But all that came later when the sad knowledge came to lodge itself uneasily in the minds of the villagers.

The women left behind were restless; Sandile's wife, Nobuntu, leading all the rest. Often her eyes wandered downhill towards the spot where the men had disappeared; where they would reappear on their way back from the river.

Although the men had left with not a word as to the nature of the trouble taking place down there, commonsense and native intuition warned Nobuntu of impending disaster. Her thoughts fastened on Jonguhlanga, the boy who had brought whatever news had sent the men flying down the hill. He was an age-mate of her son, Zama. Why had Zama not come to tell his father of a drowned animal or whatever other trouble there was down there by the river? Away galloped Nobuntu's thoughts, taking her down dark and tortured paths. Why had Mbhele's son come here to her home if her own son could have done so?

Her throat was full of all the dust the men's bare feet had beaten from the footpath, racing down towards the river. She swallowed hard and found the springs under her tongue a desert. There was a flailing frog where her heart had been.

Then a voice whispered in that heart, a voice that had lived there from the morning, long, long ago it seemed now, she had put a squalling, wrinkly-skinned bundle to her breast, and stilled it. Now, that voice stilled her fears. Wouldn't something tell her, a mother, were her only child in trouble? A flash of pain cut across her lower abdomen; reminding her of that other, years ago.

By evening, the group that had gone to scour the river came back subdued. Their feet were lead as they approached the homestead; their heads hung down. No funeral procession ever moved at slower pace.

The women saw them coming and Zama's mother, Nobuntu, started wailing. Sandile's wife wailed, although no one had told her of any death at all. She wailed, *'Uph' uZama?'* 'Where is my son?' she asked; tears marring her sight. She saw his friends, who made his absence loud. So loud she did not hear the words her mouth threw out: *'Ndixeleleni, bethuna! Uphi umntan' am? Uphi na umntan' am?'*

The other women, knowing the pain of loss, joined her; telling all within earshot the news of the death that had come like a thief, with no warning. For none had heard of an illness at the home of the old man, Zengele, father of Sandile father of Zama who, it was said in tones hushed and laced with unasked questions, had disappeared beneath the turbid waters of the River Tsomo.

Swiftly – kith, kin, friend and neighbour flocked in, to hear for themselves what grief had struck their own. And the sad tale of the drowning of Zama, Sandile's son, was told again and again and again as wave upon wave of unbelieving sympathisers came; and left shaking heads in dumbfounded gloom.

That evening, the men of the family took their sticks and went to Mbokothwane, two villages away. There was a *sangoma* there said to be the best in matters of this nature: disappearances, sudden, inexplicable deaths and accidents that might be the work of a witch. So off the men went to a *sangoma*; to hear from *she who knows* the true nature of the abomination that had befallen their home. None believed the facts as they were presented, none believed the nakedness the eye had seen. And now, in their grief, they sought illumination from those with powers and grasp beyond that of mere mortals.

And true, the *sangoma* relieved their pain.

'The boy is not dead,' she declared. She had cast her bones onto the floor and read them. And that is what the bones told her. She relayed the message from the bones to those the spirits had sent to her for help.

'He is not dead, and therefore do not grieve. Go back and say to your people, "He is not dead. Dry all your tears!"

And that is the message they brought back with them: No tears must be shed. If we shed tears, we will bring harm on him. The people who live beneath the river have taken him. They have chosen him for their own. If we follow the instructions of the *sangoma*, he will come to no harm. They mean him no harm at all, the people of the river. They want to make him theirs that he may help all people beaten down by troubles. He will be a very powerful *sangoma* when he is given back to us. But, it is imperative, absolutely imperative, that we abide by the rules set by the *sangoma*, rules she herself gets from the great spirits who rule the world we do not see; the world we cannot see with our mere human eyes.

All grieving stopped. Eyes whose lids were all puffy from weeping righted themselves. Faces tried hard to wear smiles in place of frowns. Hushed whispers were replaced by almost normal-sounding tones. And the young mother was heard humming a lullabye to her fretful baby.

That same night, the women made haste and cooked big, tall drums of mealie porridge; the first step in brewing *umqombothi* as the *sangoma* had ordered. They were even going to use yeast instead of fermenting malt; time was of the essence. Yeast clipped off two full days from the brewing process.

The next morning, a smaller number dragged its feet to the river. For the women of the family, these were days that gave not a moment's rest at the home of Zengele. If a feast were in the making there could hardly have been more for them to do. The hard beat of galloping hooves became a familiar sound as young men set off for town to get –

The liquor of the white man,
Beer that glides down the throat,
Cooling, like the waters of mountain springs;
Kicks a man to his grave
If taken without respect and circumspection.
Beer that comes in little bottles
Instead of great big vats or giant drums.
Beer that must never, never, be underestimated,
Never taken lightly or for granted!
Rare and brilliant, indeed, are Victoria's Tears!

That was the major purchase. Then there was the yeast to buy, a new sieve, vats, dishes, and an endless list of other things besides. The homestead was scoured: walls whitewashed inside and out; floors smeared fresh with cow dung; all water tanks filled with fresh water from the river; all pots washed clean, not a scrap of food remaining from the day before; and the courtyard swept clean and bare of clutter.

All day through, down by the river, the little group kept a hopeful watch. The *sangoma* had not said their child could not be sent back to them until they'd made the sacrifice. But finally, when again the sun set, the weary family went home.

The number had dwindled to all but a few stalwarts by the next day. But, this day brought nothing new either. Nothing anyone there wanted to see happen. Again, the sun went back to sleep. Again home went the family. Yet if they were daunted, they did not show it openly.

Early the fourth day, Nobuntu sprang up from her *isicamba* and with foot as light as a cat's left the *rondavel* she slept in and went to the big one in the middle. This is where all cooking was done. Here the vats of unsieved *umqombothi* waited.

The musty smell of fermented beer hit her nostrils even before she opened the door. It is ready, her nose told her. But she needed the confirmation of her eyes and tongue and so into the hut she went and up to the far wall.

The vats stood tall and brooding in the dark grey of an unlit *rondavel*, only a stray ray of moonlight thinned the pitch black of the hut. She came to the first vat, lifted the heavy sack cover, lifted the tin lid beneath it directly on the mouth of the vat. The soft swish-swish sounds that greeted her told her: it is done! She grabbed a scoop from the near-by table and dipped it sideways into the vat, stirring lightly. When her hand told her she had broken past the crusty fer-mented malt and hit the thickish liquid, she righted the scoop and brought it first to her nose and sniffed, taking a long slow draw of breath. Then to her mouth. A deep sip. Smack, went her lips. The verdict was good. The *umqombothi* was ready. Again, she covered the vat she had opened.

Outside the moon painted the village a ghostly white. But that didn't stop Nobuntu. Taking a pail, she went down to the river. Before she prepares food of a morning, a good woman goes to the river to wash. Her mother had told her that – long ago when she was as high as a dog. Today, those truths buried deep in her brain led her on. About to sieve *umqombothi* for the affair of her son, Nobuntu did all she knew how, to satisfy herself and any who cared that she played by the rules.

Zama's mother did not tarry long at the river. She had a full day ahead. A day that would bring her much joy. But first, there was work to be done. She had washed herself and filled her pail with water. She hastened up the incline not feeling the full pail on her head as a weight at all. Her head was used to carrying water or wood: she had done that since before her breasts had even sprouted.

Back in the middle hut, she took an empty drum and brought it close to the vats of beer. She plugged the drum with a metal sieve, uncovered one of the vats and plunged a long wooden ladle into the frothing, swishing beer. Warm, yeasty aroma hit her nose. With the metal scoop, she took beer from the vat and poured it into the sieve on top of the drum – three or four times. The sieve was almost full. Then she began to stir the beer in the sieve with her right hand going to and fro flat but lightly against the bottom of the sieve. And the beer ran through the sieve and hit the bottom of the drum and made the most amazing noises. Each time the sieve ran out of beer and had just the chaff left, Nobuntu scooped out the chaff and, between her hands, squeezed it of all moisture and then threw it into an empty tin waiting nearby. Then she began the process all over again. The noises of the drum continued but changed tone with the rising of the level of the beer in the drum – changed from loud, raucous sharps to dulled humming until, nearly full, the drum sank into a contented, swollen silence. Only the keenest ear, close up and strained to the limit, would have heard the hint of a purr the beer now gave.

In the grey light of morning, one by one, the women came to help sieve the *umqombothi*, giving Nobuntu some well-earned rest. Before long, several drums of *umqombothi* stood tall and proud. And happily full. Happily full. Now the younger women took the vats into the courtyard and rinsed them free of stray strands of malt. From the metal drums, back into the vats went the beer. Vats are better for storing *umqombothi*, the villagers said. The wood gives the beer body and keeps it cooler than metal.

The men too, had things to see to this day. There was a beast to be chosen for the ceremony, the best among the oxen of the *kraal*. The slaughtering of a beast is an essential part of all ceremonies; especially those that have anything to do with communication with the spirits: be it in appeasement, thanksgiving or praise – blood must be spilled.

Zengele had given the word:

'Take the fattest ox with the sleekest coat for my grandson.' Urging them to be careful, he warned, 'And be sure it is in no way flawed.'

Why would he want to insult the All Powerful who live

beneath the water? And, even were he that stupid, why now, with Zama's life hanging in the balance?

In the middle of the hectic activity, came Reverend Mazwi of the Holy Abyssinian Church in Africa. Hearing of the drowning of the young brother-in-the-Lord, he had taken a hasty breakfast and set off to visit the afflicted family, members of his flock.

He came armed with words of condolence; words with which he would bind the bleeding wounds of the bereaved family. In his mind were no doubts. The young man had drowned. He was dead. There was also no doubt in the mind of the humble servant of the living God that he had a duty – to help begin the healing of his sorrowing brethren.

Was he ever horrified therefore, to find members of his congregation reverting to heathenish practices!

'How can you do these disgraceful things? Do you not fear the wrath of God?' Thunder erupted from his mouth. In vain, he tried to talk the family out of the whole thing; now pleading, now threatening, and now striking a balance somewhere between the two; on his brow a thick, dark cloud.

When he saw that Christian admonitions helped not at all, the minister appealed to sound economic reason: 'Why waste so much money dear Brother-in-the-Living-Christ? Your ox? How can you sacrifice your fatted ox because of the crazy ramblings of an ignorant woman? How can you pay heed to the rantings of a Jezebel; a whore ruled by the devil?'

But Zengele stood firm. Even when the Reverend Minister threatened to expel from his congregation all those who took part, in whatever manner, in the rites under way, the old man would not budge.

As well the man of God directed his appeals to Zengele. He was the village elder, head of his family, and the family could not but obey him. Their loyalty was of that kind. Simple. The word of the elders, law.

The careful words of consolation in the minister's chest shrivelled; scorched by the stubborn, dry eyes that refused to grieve, eyes that did not accept the death he had come to lament but cherished the hope planted in their hearts by the *sangoma*.

'You are all in the employ of the Devil! *Niziqeshise ngoMtyholi!*' Shouting, the minister left, taking with him a few who preferred to wear their faith like a head covering, without which no grown man or woman ever leaves the house.

The beer was sieved and frothing and spilling over the brims of two vast vats. Brand new. As far as possible, everything had to be new. Who would dare deliver food to the gods in tarnished dishes?

Against the far wall, rows and rows of bottles of brandy stood gleaming; paying homage at the foot of the vats of beer.

In the *kraal*, the ox stood alone; he had been kept from going to the *veld*. Now and then he bellowed; his lush coat shimmering in the bright, shadow-shrinking sun of noon. At each bellow, those within ear-shot cried out, '*CAMAGU!*' For the bellow of the ox was a sign the gods looked favourably on the sacrifice. '*CAMAGU!*'

An ox must be slaughtered, right there by the river. That is what the *sangoma* had said. And now, in song, hope lending a spring to their gait, the swelling hordes danced their way to the appointed place. The *sangoma* had said the spirits would sense any reluctance, any begrudging, any sadness. The family purged their hearts of all such untoward feelings.

It was time to go; to take the offering to the river gods. On the heads of maidens, the virgins of the clan, vats stood tall and full. Young men took turns shouldering the two boxes of brandy bottles. Down to the river went Zengele's family accompanied by friends, sympathizers, and all and sundry. At the head of the group, Nobuntu and her husband, Sandile, walked as in a dream. There was much singing, much clapping of hands and stamping of feet as the group approached the place where Zama was last seen. But Nobuntu and her husband were subdued. The whole procession appeared to them as some distant thing from which someone might shake them awake, a nightmare not to be believed.

On the banks of the river, the ox was slaughtered. No bone was broken; the only blood allowed to spill from the ruptured jugular vein was collected in a new bowl and then poured into a bottle as clean as clean could be. Not a morsel was taken, all the meat, enfolded in the skin, was thrown into the river '... at that very spot where he went down' as the *sangoma* had instructed.

Down that same spot, went the bottles of Queen Victoria's tears. Only *umqombothi* did the people drink as they stood watching the spot from which he would emerge; the same spot where he had gone down. 'The same, same, very same spot.' That is what the *sangoma* had told them. That is what she had said.

Reverend Mazwi and the men who had left Zengele's home with him in utter disgust quickly spread word of the horror that was 'greater than the disaster that had struck Zengele's home.' By noon, the whole village knew of the wayward ways of that family 'who still believed in things of darkness and went to *izangoma*.'

That whole day, the entire village talked of nothing else. Have you heard? Neighbour asked neighbour. Have you heard? Parent asked offspring and young people of all ages, girls and boys asked each other and one another: Have you heard? Have you heard? Have you heard?

'Is that right, now?' asked some, looking askance at the display of such dire ignorance. Others shrugged shoulders saying, 'We shall see. We shall see.' Clearly foreseeing results quite different from those Zengele's family were buying, at such a price. 'They are wasting their time and money,' said less circumspect sceptics. 'Who takes a man to court because he slaughters his own ox?' the bold came right out and asked. 'Do they really believe that someone who drowned, three days gone, can live again just because they slaughter an ox?'

A young man, an activist, shook his head in disbelief. 'I give up on my people,' he mourned. 'They will never tire of believing in Nongqawuse,' he lamented; referring to the 1857 episode where *amaXhosa* were duped into killing all their cattle. However, the majority of the villagers believed in what Zengele was doing. Only, only among like-minded others would they have openly admitted that they did.

Imperceptibly, the sun went along its course, due west. But the crowd sang right on, hands clapping a racket and feet beating a storm from the hard, bare ground while the people awaited the promised miracle. Their voices grew hoarse, their spirits never wavered, their hopes did not dwindle. They drank *umqombothi* and kept up the vigil.

The sun had long gone to sleep when they finally decided they should go home to return the next morning. The spirits would not send the boy back by night, they told themselves. These were spirits of light not demons, evil spirits of the dark. Thus consoled, they left, certain they would see their son rise from the river the next morning. They would be there to see it happen. They had not even reached Zengele's home when another group, smaller in number and more youthful, happened on the same, same scene. The young men, students from the local teacher-training college, hearing of the ceremony, had come to watch. However, they had taken great care not to be seen, hiding among the trees and shrubs bordering the river.

The celebrants gone, there developed an argument among the students. There were those who wanted to retrieve the meat and liquor from the river. However, a few considered such an act sacrilegious, a desecration of the ceremony and sacrifice of a family, and they would have no part of it.

'As it is, we were probably wrong even to come and watch,' Vusumzi said, 'but that is as far as I will go.' And, breaking cover, he set his nose towards the school hostel.

'Aarh, let him go!' urged Mthetho, championing the cause of the retrievers. But some of the young men followed Vusumzi although one or two among them looked a little sheepish.

'Yes, let them go!' Lunga, Mthetho's lieutenant, agreed. 'There will be more for us then,' he added in gleeful anticipation.

'God always provides,' reiterated Mthetho, encouraged by Lunga's support. 'But we must not make the mistake of thinking we will see His hand when He gives us something. As our forebears used to say, His ways are not our ways and He doesn't give by hand as we do.'

'And remember what is waiting for you back at the boarding-school dining hall!' shouted one of the group, choosing to do so anonymously.

The diet at the boarding-school, *calico* six days a week and Sundays, a snip of third-grade meat less than an inch whichever way one measured it, was a constant irritation of long standing to the boarders. And as soon as the group was reminded of the fact, all wavering left even the most hesitant among those who had remained. If there was one among the group whose morality bothered him, he was not that stupid he would make himself unpopular by going against the wishes of the majority. And Mthetho was a one-man majority of substance. He enjoyed the adoration of the entire school.

Three boys, the best swimmers among the group, crept along and down the banks of the river, and dived deep down where they had seen all that good meat go down. And all that liquor! Surely, the gods were smiling down on them. The others, keeping a sharp look out, cheered each time one of the divers came up, hands laden with loot.

Early next morning the faithful returned to the river, their eyelids peeled. None wanted to miss a thing. So certain were they that the swirling waters would regurgitate Zama that, as they neared the river, a few of the women broke out in wild ululation.

Song and dance waned, however, the higher and bolder the sky's red eye rose. By the time it told schoolchildren to go home, voices were hoarse from the strain of days and days of unending hollering. But the bigger strain was fighting the doubt gnawing at many hearts. Doubt none dared admit. Only the insane would risk the ire of the river gods. Only the demented would jeopardise the very life they so treasured and were there to salvage. So each morning, faithfully, their hope rising with the passing days – how could the river gods keep him down there for ever? How long will they go on testing us? – we kept our end of the bargain.

At the boarding-school the startling change that had come over some of the boys had not gone unnoticed. Boys hitherto known to be voracious, cheerfully spurned the offerings from the school's kitchen. To the amazed delight of the Boarding Master, however, a cheerful mood accompanied this inexplicable trend that had descended on some of his young wards. He prayed the mood would last; he had eight more months to go; come December, he was retiring. On the fertile slopes of the Tsitsa River, his mealie farm awaited him. There he would spend the rest of his days in peace, tending to his crops.

His Assistant, however, was of a more inquisitive nature and liked to get to the bottom of any mystery; especially where the boarders were concerned. Two or three of the jolly group he called into his office. And, sure enough, didn't he catch a whiff of liquor on the breath of all of them?

In no time at all, the Assistant Boarding Master had a full confession.

The sun's rays were strong and long, spearing people right on the head and stripping man, tree, and house bare of all shadow when the Assistant Boarding Master went to Zengele's home with the culprits.

'They have all gone to the river,' the old woman minding the pots told the group from the Teacher Training College. Six days running, she had been left alone. She prayed to her gods that today they would bring the child back. Six days. Even if Zama had died, his gall bladder would have burst by now. Let them bring him back. The uncertainty would kill her otherwise. With a jolt, the old woman saw that the people from the big school were still there, waiting. Quickly, she unscrambled her thoughts and repeated the words she had already given them: They have all gone to the river. And then remembered she had more words in her head that she could give to them: 'Because of the matter of this child, Zama.' And down that way the Master took his wards.

Short, strong shadows were beginning to appear, all pointing east, as this small group came within a few metres of that part of the river where Zengele and his family, friends, wellwishers and the plainly curious were gathered. Just then, a scream split the day, sending dogs into a frenzy.

Zama's body had come bobbing up to the surface of the water.

Six days after he had last been seen alive, as he went head first into a clear pool that was far from deep, the body of the young man was found, caught by the ankle in a craggy outcrop of mossy boulders more than two hundred metres away from the spot where the family had sent down their sacrifice and danced four long days singing themselves hoarse.

Before shock-widened eyes, one of the young men waded

into the shallows and, in his dripping arms, brought Zama ashore. More than two hundred metres below the spot where the hope-filled family had buried the meat and the liquor, that is where the body was found. Far below the same, same spot where the boy was seen going down. The spot from which, according to the *sangoma*, the spirits of the river would send him back. But that is not the spot where his body did come up. Not the same spot at all.

This new development threw the Assistant Boarding Master into a tease. He had to think of the reputation of the school. What good could possibly come of revealing the boys' misdemeanour now? And there was the real danger such an action might just turn the community against the school. Feelings were likely to run high; never a condition for clear thinking. The simple minds of village folk would just heap condemnation on the school, accuse it of lack of proper supervision. People had no idea how difficult it was to run a boarding-school. Clearly, the Assistant Boarding Master's discretion dictated protecting the goodwill the school enjoyed among the general populace.

The family, stricken, blamed no one. 'These things happen,' they said and accepted the verdict of the *sangoma* ... and understood. How could they blame anyone? 'Are we gods that we can be such masters of our feelings that we can completely erase grief and fear?' Their minds groped in painful confusion. 'So, the river spirits had been affronted. In their displeasure, they had left the boy in the water unprotected and...he succumbed.' To themselves they explained the plainly inexplicable, deciphered the stabbing mystery.

Whom could they blame? Whoever had not been able to kill the sorrow in the heart, they were convinced, had been incapacitated only by a great, great love. A mother's tender heart for her only child? A young lover's inexperienced heart? A father's doubting heart? How could they ever know?

Rumour of the schoolboys' mischief surfaced soon after Zama's funeral. But most people in the village, especially the bereaved, did not take the rumour seriously; they did not believe such a thing could happen. Would even the children of school be that disrespectful, risk measureless abomination, desecrate a family's supplication? What wretch of a fool would invite the wrath of the ancestors like that?

Not a few of the villagers saw the hand of a *mthakathi*, in the whole fishy affair. 'Don't tell me anything, it's plain to see someone did Zama in. How d'you think anyone that age and size could drown in a mere washing-basin of water? *Suka! Ulunjiwe!*'

Sceptics had a field day. Not exactly gloating, they said – 'Even if those boys had not fished out the sacrifice, the outcome would have been the same.'

And there were those who believed the whole thing was doomed. Why had nobody told Zengele a sacrificial beast must not have even a fleck of black? 'The left eyelid of that ox he used was black,' they said. 'So, what do you expect when people will be that careless?'

House-Hunting Unlike Soweto

I find the whole thing bewildering, I must confess. Not just coming to the United States, after all, this was my third trip to the country. But this time I was not just bringing myself, I was not coming at the invitation of the State Department, furnished with an escort. Neither was I coming as a student to be sheltered in students' dorms, enlightened by student advisors, and have my stay monitored by the time-tested mechanisms of a sound, world-renowned institution. This time, I was at the head of a five-member delegation, my family – my four children and I. The hurricane of the schools boycott had driven me to these shores, so now, what did I expect? What was I in search of? What dreams were pinned inside the hems of my petticoats?

While our children were busy boycotting classes, the time God set was wilfully going on its own sweet accord. My children, each one of them five years behind in her or his education, were five years ahead in age in any class you'd put them into. *MISFITS*. There was no kinder way of putting it. The kindest, most sympathetic principal in the City of New York could not just take them and put them into a class. Everything about them was just so wrong: *especially the age*. They were all too old for the classes they were supposed to be in.

On top of that, we had no records of their immunization. Records? Records are kept when there are recognized people to whom those records pertain. In a country where the citizenship of the African was not recognized, why would the government have taken the trouble to keep records that showed that a child of mine had been given this or that immunization? In fact, why would that child be immunized at all? Wouldn't that be counter-productive to the grand plan of culling our numbers – by hook or by crook?

If the education of my children was a key factor in our leaving South Africa, finding accommodation was priority after our arrival in New York. Where does a poor soul with no experience – first, second, or any other hand – of looking for accommodation begin doing that in of all places the Big Apple? Forty years old, I wondered.

No, I was not a member of a newly discovered tribe of mountain-dwellers. Neither had I spent my entire life in a mental asylum. I was fresh from a country where, despite my protestation, at times even vigorous, the government insisted on 'protecting' me from the vagaries of modern living, including real estate.

In South Africa before the changes after 1990, urban Africans lived in townships. However, not every African had the right to rent a house (buying was out of the question, illegal). And until recently, only a man could get permission to rent. On condition he 'qualified' for residence in the particular urban area; he was married; his wife also 'qualified' for residential purposes in the same urban area. It helped the couple's cause greatly if they already had children.

But I, being a woman, never had the shadow of a chance of renting a house although I 'qualified' for residential and work purposes in the Prescribed Area of the Western Cape. Moreover, when I married, I had committed the folly of choosing a man allowed only to work in Cape Town – a migrant labourer.

But that was long ago, in another life. Now, I had left South Africa. New York had no Bantu Administration

Boards to regulate every aspect of my life. How do normal people get to live in normal houses, I asked, first myself and then others.

'You have to go through the Real Estate pages of the newspaper or go to a Real Estate Agent,' advised friends, little realizing they might as well tell me to read hieroglyphics.

The Real Estate Section of the paper, in South Africa, is about that ... real estate; it has nothing at all to do with the squalid matchboxes we had been forced to live in in the African townships. Therefore, this is a section of the paper that we, Africans, did not look at. Why would we have bothered looking into that section since we were not allowed to live in those areas with houses that got themselves listed there?

I had never set eyes on the financial section, the vacations section, or the leisure section – for the same or a similar reason: exclusion, whether legal or economic. Thus did I discover the extent of my deprivation. Here I was, one of the lucky few among my people, part of the one per cent or so who had somehow escaped government design, our planned dwarfing, and I could make neither head nor tail of a section of the newspaper; so sucessfully had I been bonsaid.

After wading through numerous Real Estate sections and with hefty help from several kindly colleagues from the office, I was afire: If I save, I told myself, in two years I will have $20 000 and buy a house on Fifth Avenue!

Greatly encouraged, I began building my American castle. However, as this was clearly a long-term objective, I kept on scanning the paper, looking for somewhere to stay. My heart quickened at this description: Three bedrooms, including Master Bedroom, two full baths, separate dining room, eat-in kitchen; 24-hour doorman service. Perfect! The jacuzzi was but the crowning glory.

My heart racing, I reached for the phone.

'I'm interested in the three-bedroom you advertise in

today's *New York Times*,' I cooed with what I hoped was my
most unfathomable but intriguing accent, evocative of diplo-
matic links and unlimited wealth.

'Are you calling from the city, Ma'm?' And when I replied
that I was, this highly polished voice, warm and reassuring,
demanded – 'When would you like to see it?'

'Oh, this afternoon ... say, three – three-thirty. If that's all
right with you? Then, as an afterthought, I ventured, 'By the
way, how much is the rent?'

Quick came the retort, 'If you have to ask that question,
then you can't afford it.' Gone was the friendly tone; the
voice temperature had dropped a clear ten degrees!

Several similarly futile attempts later, I deemed it best to
pursue the apartment on Fifth Avenue even though it had no
alluring bathroom features. I foresaw no insurmountable
problems in raising a mortgage. 'This is the US of A, I can do
anything like everybody else,' I told myself dialling the number.

'Two months' rent is required as security. Of course, this
goes into an interest-bearing account.'

An alarm went off in my head. Something was radically
wrong. Why was this man talking about rent, about security?

I no longer recall most of what this particular agent said
by way of explanation. My ears had taken unscheduled
leave; my brain reduced to cornmeal porridge. *TWENTY
THOUSAND DOLLARS!* I had difficulty seeing the figure
in my mind's eye. *$20 000!* Not the sale price. Not the down
payment or deposit. No. This was the monthly rental. I did-
n't make that much money in six months! The whole of me
boggled. I broke out into a cold sweat. This piece of information was just too much for me to digest – that there were
people out there who not only made that kind of money,
each month; but made so much that they could spend, on
rent alone, $20 000 per month.

As straw to a drowning man, conventional wisdom sprang to the rescue: *Cut your coat according to your cloth!* came unbidden to my mind.

But the real lesson, the full brunt of the 'benevolence' of a government that had painstakingly 'sheltered' me, was only then beginning to unfold.

My coat, I saw with brutal clarity, was going to have to be a cheap rental. Very cheap. After a brief search, I found something suitable. Less than a week after we'd moved in, I also learnt why the rent was that low. There is a bit more to looking for accommodation than affordability alone. The apartment I had rented was located in that part of the Bronx where the film *Fort Apache* was shot.

All around were rotting, burn-blackened buildings; a thick pall of foulness strangled the very air; gaunt, misshappen human frames in tatters aimlessly roamed the streets all day long, and all night through; the whole place displayed ample evidence of total decay, scars from ancient battles.

It is here that the term 'danger money' assumed new meaning for us as a family. I insisted on each child carrying, separately, two ten dollar bills: one, to give to a mugger in the event of being accosted by one; and the other, to hop into a cab if lost or in a threatening situation. This had nothing to do with dating and I gave this sum to the boys as well as to the girls. Never mind that I discovered later my gang used the money as extra pocket money, for they had made their own discovery: their poor old mother had finally gone soft in the head. Before six months and although we had a one-year lease, we fled that far from that cosy nest.

I found a sublet in a Co-op building. Two months later, we had to leave. I was paying both rent and storage for my furniture, which had not been allowed into the building. What did I know of Board approval? I did not even know there were such things Co-op Boards.

Our next castle was also a co-op. But, wiser now, I had

insisted on, and received, the approval of the Board before moving in. The rent was going to be $100 less for the first month because the place badly needed painting. During that time the landlady promised to have that done while I kept my furniture in storage; hence the deduction in rent.

Four months later, the workmen had become permanent fixtures in 'my' home. The project had insidiously expanded. The lady was putting lights in the closets, changing the ceiling light fixtures, adding scones to the walls, replastering the walls, and putting new faucets in the bathroom and kitchen sinks. All commendable, no doubt. However, the constant drilling and chipping, hammering and scraping and the droning of machines furiously at work, drove us all up the wall. The constant assault of foul, acidic smells penetrated every niche, nook and cranny of the apartment and glued themselves into our clothes and our very hair. We could taste them on our teeth, I swear. But above all, the intrusion of the workmen into our lives became an unbearable irritation. In short, this work, necessary, no doubt, should never have been done while the place was occupied. I had a mighty fight with the landlady and withheld part of the rent, telling her, 'We are taking our clothes to the cleaners with it.' You know how it is when you are desperately unhappy about a situation? It is the one topic you cannot leave alone. At work, on the subway, at the office, I talked about nothing else. To total strangers at times. Of course, there is nothing people like better than giving advice. And I became the recipient of much and varied counsel from concerned veterans of Real Estate Battles.

'If you are thinking of moving into a certain neighbourhood,' said my eager advisors, 'go there at different times: week days, weekends, early mornings, late at night.

'A place can look fine with the morning rush – school kids and people going to work, you know? But you don't know what comes creeping out during the day.'

'Check the public transportation. You don't want to be far from buses and the subway. And you definitely want to watch out you do not end up in a two-fare zone. That adds to your expenses.'

'A good indicator is if you find long-term real estate near by: schools and church buildings. Those don't go away and the neighbourhoods where you find them are less likely to go to the dogs in a hurry.'

Unfortunately, this sound advice came a little late to save me, beleaguered from many fronts as I was. Moving is expensive in New York; a far cry from home where one calls on friends and neighbours to lend a hand. In New York, movers are hired and they don't come cheap. So, we had to tarry longer than we would have liked at this place because I needed to recuperate, financially, from the previous moves, chasing each other as they did.

Eventually though, we did move. And the younger of my two sons stopped saying 'Thugs willing!' in response to my 'See you soon,' as I left for work or went jogging or food shopping.

Now, we live in a good neighbourhood. I no longer worry about the safety of my children. But that is not to say that everything is honky-dorry now. The children have had quite a hard time adjusting. Of course, they want to be like the other young people here; they don't want to be different. I think it's harder for me, watching them change; seeing the people I knew become others, very different from what I had envisaged.

Remember, when I had these children I had a very different set of beliefs, different expectations, and I was in a different world. I was going to get *lobola* for my daughters, one day. And here I am, getting used to the idea that no young man's family will come and meet with members of my family; enter into negotiations, give us *lobola*; and then, and only then, marry my daughter. No. My daughters' weddings will be individual affairs: between 'two consenting adults' and I will be lucky if someone remembers to inform me – not ask for my permission, no. Inform me she is getting married. To a man I might not know from a bar of soap!

I am a mother to daughters who can now bring young men into my house, boyfriends. And I welcome that. Families have lost daughters in this country because the young man simply killed the girl. Just like that. So, for the safety of my daughters, I allow what was an abomination in my youth to take place in my house. A man who has given no *lobola* for my daughter comes into my house; when my people have not set eyes on his people. This child whom I bore and nursed, with whom I sat up long nights when she was ill, this child is now a free gift to some man who promises me nothing, nothing at all. And cares little about me and the people of whom I am part; of whom the young woman he will marry is a part. One day, I will have grandchildren who will not know my language or my customs, whose ways will not be the ways of my people. Truly, it is a never-ending journey that I have undertaken. The children are getting their education in this country. But, so am I. Although mine will not come with any certificates. So am I ... getting quite an education.

Push-Push!

Like a veld fire, the fever swept through Blouvlei; putting a jaunty spring to the gait of old men. It painted a glint in the eyes of housewives and made husbands tremble – filled with lust for the wealth and with dire trepidation for the power it might bestow on their up-to-now docile wives. Surely, that could happen were a man to be foolish enough to allow his wife to go it alone.

The whole of Blouvlei was astir. Wealth had come a-knocking at the door of each family there. Equal opportunity. Poverty, that invisible guest intimate to all Blouvlei dwellers, was about to be banished from their homes – for ever.

Push-Push! Push-Push! Push-Push! sounded the siren call. And like the children of Hamelin Town in Brunswick, the residents responded with gleeful abandon.

The scheme was so simple many wondered why they had not thought about it themselves. 'It's a pyramid,' explained the men who brought such glittering prospects to this sprawling location of rickety, rust-brown tin shacks, where modernity, a mere two or three kilometres away, had failed to penetrate. 'You put your money into the common fund and, as others put theirs after you, their money pushes yours up and up and up and up – till it gets to the very top!' That is how those in the know explained the affair.

However, that was not the end. Would the whole of Blouvlei have been sizzling just for that? No. As it made its journey to the top of the pyramid, the money grew and grew and grew. It accumulated more money: Profit. Gain. Interest. No one paid particular attention to the preciseness of the terms. 'It breeds,' said Blouvlei's benefactors, beaming from ear to ear.

There was a mad scramble as people cast their hands everywhere in search of money – always a scarce commodity in their lives.

Push-Push! Push-Push! Here was a chance to escape poverty once and for all. Who was deaf? Not the people whose idea of splurging was tripe on a week day and *skaap-kop* for Sunday dinner. All one had to do, was cough up three or four or five hundred Rands. That's all. 'And your money will come back multiplied ten times!'

'*Ikhiwa ngezikotile!* It is being scooped up in dishes!' resounded the thrilling testimony, music to the ear. Even people who'd never set foot in school learnt the ten times multiplication table overnight.

Domestic workers, suddenly the envy of house-bound housewives, borrowed money from their madams – most against future earnings. Men, heads of families, mortgaged wages of two years and more, so searing was the dream of today: abundance unprecedented, about to be thrust into their eager, outstretched hands. People borrowed from the church, from the teachers of their children; parents from working children, friends from each other (and, indeed, sometimes from people they had but recently regarded as less than friend). It was hard to come across one person in Blouvlei who had not been bitten by the Push-Push bug.

One woman stumbled on the astounding fact that her husband, unable to raise funds any other way, was negotiating the sale of their three-year-old son to a childless couple. The bewildered woman fled to relatives in the Ciskei taking the little boy with her.

Every neighbourhood has its sceptic. In Blouvlei, this diabolical monster housed itself in the body of my father. An otherwise kind and reasonable soul, this gentleman had an in-born suspicion of all money that did not come in an envelope with his name on it – an envelope received from the hands of a white man on a Friday, unless that day fell on a holiday. Then the envelope might come a day or two later. In the midst of the frenzy, father refused to be drawn in. He was not about to get up in the middle of some nameless, moonless night, open the window wide and fling his hard-earned money away through it. 'And then sit back, waiting for whoever happened to pick it up to not only return it to me, its rightful owner, NO. This madman, before doing that, must also, out of the kindness of his heart, take money from his own pocket and add that to the money a fool he does not know from a bar of soap decided to throw to the midnight winds.'

Mother wilted under this new tribulation. 'Oh, me. Why did I ever marry such a miser; so slow to catch on, he's always missing out.' And on one occasion, the cause of her sorrow present, she cajoled: 'Opportunity can only knock, you know, Father of Nozimbo? You have to open the door to let it in. Why are you so slow, always?'

Showing no sign that he had heard the vexation in his wife's voice or noticed that that voice was pitched several decibels above normal, father responded with characteristic equanimity, 'Let's wait and see.'

Visibly, mother puffed herself up as a toad sensing an enemy. Now, she was screaming: 'You're such a ...! Such a ...' For once lost for words, she blurted: 'Such a Slow Coach!' And the label stuck. So fitting.

I have never loved my father less than during this most trying period. Of all the misfortune that can be piled on a little girl's head: we would be the laughing stock of all of Retreat – not just Blouvlei. Slow Coach and his lack of vision! While even the lame and the blind were busy getting rich, the deaf responding to the call with alacrity, he, with his usual backwardness, still needed explanations. He wanted proof and time 'to think this whole thing through'. Lord! We would be the only family left without having benefited from such bounteousness. If I had the money, I thought miserably, I'd gladly give it all to Mama who would put it into the Push-Push fund. When it returned (of course, there would be so much more), we'd leave Slow Coach here, all alone in his wretched poverty. That was what he wanted and, as far as I was concerned, he could keep it all to himself. Right now, however, the situation was that Mama and I were stuck with him. Unfortunately.

People were getting rich by the day, from Mama's sullen, regret-filled reports: 'MaNdlovu and her husband. They got five hundred Rands, today! And what had they put in? What had they put in, d'you want to know? A lousy one hundred rands. That's all!'

No one was bothered by the inconsistencies. There was neither rhyme nor reason to the payoffs. Just because MaNdlovu was given five hundred rands for her investment of one hundred it did not necessarily follow that another, putting in the same amount, would receive equitable returns. The waiting period, too, differed from person to person.

Of course, Father was quick to notice the discrepancies. 'Didn't you tell me MaMkhwemnte had put in one hundred too and that she received more than a thousand Rands?'

'Well, maybe she had more people pushing her. Don't ask me things over which I have no control. Am I not the one whose wise husband won't put any money in Push-Push? How must I know how the thing works if I'm not in it?'

I was not in it either, but I too had noticed that, according to Mama's own reports, not everyone got back ten times what they had put in. However, I judged it best to keep that observation to myself. Father certainly needed no additional weapons to use in holding us back. In my opinion, he already had enough in his arsenal.

'*Ntombi yam*, my daughter,' said Mama one day her voice choking with regret and envy. It killed her to watch others getting rich while she, poor woman, stood helplessly looking on. '*Ungaze ubhalise imali yakho ngegama lendoda!* Never have your money (written) registered in a man's name.'

Just before the advent of Push-Push, Mama and Tata had taken the enlightened and daring step of putting their money in a savings account. No, not in a bank. Blouvlei people knew nothing about banks and thought the people who worked there, 'the bank people', were millionaires, owners of those banks and everyone else who set foot there, likewise endowed. They had put their money in a Post Office Savings Book. In Father's name. Although it was Mama's money. All of it.

Mama never worked. She had more money than Father who did. He worked long, very long hours. Left the house at four-thirty in the morning and usually we wouldn't see him till well after dark. There were days he returned long after bedtime. And days he didn't come back at all, sometimes for a stretch: a week or two at a time. Overtime. He earned a little more money that way.

However, the engine that drove our family, kept it going, relentlessly so, was Mother.

As long as I remember, Mama has always done something to help out. But, for some reason, the things Mama did to supplement the family's meagre income were never called work. Perhaps this is because she did them at home and didn't have to get all dressed up or put on a uniform to do them. Things which Father, a petrol attendant, did.

Mama sold *vetkoek*, *frikkadels*, gingerbeer, and sweets. Always, but always, the small, one-room house we called home wore the unshakable air of an indoor market: food smells and other living smells of the poor filled the house day and night. Yeasty smells, musty smells, and fishy smells. You found them all in our house. From frying *vetkoek*; stewing *isityhwentywe* (innards with a soupçon of vegetables); hot fish oil cooling before being used again; yeast and grease. All these smells came to our house, felt most welcome there and stayed on to become comfortable sub-tenants. I never knew there was such a thing as a house where the people in it didn't spend half their waking hours shooing away flies from food, from the exposed parts of their bodies, and from the house itself when visitors were expected.

But what use to her now, all that hard-earned money, money from the sweat of her brow? In her hour of direst need, was it not safely stashed away at the Post Office? Was it not there not in her name but in that of her husband, Slow Coach?

The injustice of it all. Here was Mama who made more money than Father, but her hands were tied. And, as a result of that, we would miss out on heaven.

Young as I was, I was well aware of the extraordinary nature of the event. I had never heard of anyone, except perhaps in *iintsomi*, our folktales, getting rich with the amazing swiftness we were witnessing in Blouvlei during those giddy days.

But, 'Slow Coach' was still painfully groping for understanding. He wanted to know exactly how '… those who push the ones that get all this plenty' would be compensated. 'Where will their ten-fold, their magnificent abundance, hail from?', he queried, to Mama's exasperation and my despair and humiliation. Of course, I knew, all my friends wouldn't want to play with me once they were rich. As surely all of them would be. Soon. I would be an outcast; a leper whom all former playmates shunned. How could even Father do this to us? My anguish knew no end.

And then, at last, even the sceptic succumbed. Mama would not let up and the pressure finally cracked Father open, wide as the Grand Canyon.

In some things, however, it is wiser to leap before looking, wiser to be among the first. That was definitely the case with Push-Push.

We were doomed to be among the last; thanks, once again, to ... Slow Coach. We would be the broad base of the pyramid that remains forever stuck in the ground whilst the apex kissed the clouds up there. We never made it to the promised land.

We pushed too late when none were left to push us forward or upward – towards our own ten-fold wealth. Unfortunately, when we eventually did decide to push, we also decided to do so with all we had. At any rate, that is what I surmised from my parent's frequent and bitter exchanges; a new phenomenon. Arguments I was used to, but before this they had no bitterness in them. And were rather rare.

Like the proverbial thief who steals away by night, the leader of the gentlemen who had brought the prophecy to the Africans of the locations of Cape Town, a schoolteacher, my own teacher whom I loved with all the intensity of an eleven-year-old schoolgirl's heart, had disappeared without a trace; nailing my poor parents forever in that unenviable state we were so desperate to escape; bequeathing them perpetual recriminations.

The flutter and flurry was frightening. My family was by no means the only one thus swindled. The magnitude of the fraud was unbelievable, once it came to light. Hundreds of people had gambled away their entire life's savings, others had acquired enormous debt whilst there were those who, certain they would replace it before any detected it was missing, had used money entrusted to them for safekeeping.

Gong-Gong! Gong-Gong! Gong-Gong! The rude beat of wood on metal sounded early one morning, pulling people from their wobbly beds and out of their tumbledown shacks. Outside, no thudding of feet greeted them, for sand swallows all sound. But up and down that untarred terrain came the hordes bearing bad news.

Push-Push! Push-Push! Voices raised in holy ire. Push-Push! Push-Push! *Imali kaPush-Push imkile!* Women screamed the warning: Gone is the Push-Push money! Throughout the length and breadth of Blouvlei, beating sticks on empty, four-gallon paraffin tins, raising the alarm, calling the faithful to a mass meeting, marched the hearts and feet of angry women; their dreams turning to dust right before their very eyes.

By mid-morning, hundreds converged on the common, a sandy patch of open ground replete with twigs, broken bottles, bones, scraps of paper, pieces of cardboard, assorted bits and pieces of clothing, peel and other fall-out from meal preparations as well as vestiges of meals from yesteryear. They were all gathered there in vain attempt to find the culprit and recoup their losses.

That evening Mama told Father that a meeting had been called regarding the disappearance of the Push-Push men. 'I have to go to work tomorrow,' Father bellowed, refusing to go to the meeting. An I-told-you-so look sat on his suddenly tired eyes. So Mother went to the meeting without him.

At school the next day classes were disrupted as wrathful residents marched on the school.

'We want the crook! Give him to us! We want the crook! Give him to us!' they chanted.

'Push-Push!', some hollered. 'Let us have him and we'll push him straight through to Hell!'

We were sent home although it was before morning break. Later, we heard that the teachers had had a hard time convincing the angry mob that the teacher they sought was not at school. 'As soon as we have knowledge of his whereabouts we shall convey that knowledge to you,' promised the School Inspector, Mr Swanepoel. That august personage had been hastily summoned from the Circuit Office in Cape Town.

That whole week, classes were an uneasy, iffy affair. The people of Blouvlei were up in arms, in and out of the school at all times; trying to surprise the miscreant, unwilling to accept he had absconded from his teaching post.

A pall settled over Blouvlei; all laughter stopped and smiles were scarce. For months thereafter, when asked, '*Ninjani?* How are you?', residents there would reply, 'Except for this abomination that has befallen us, you know? The man who has swallowed our money and then was himself swallowed by the ground; well, except for that, I suppose I can say we are doing fine.' Not a few openly expressed their desire to take him alive and slice him into thin, thin, shreds '... that even one who knows him intimately would not recognize.' They asserted, 'Just killing such a dog would be too kind. First, one must let him suffer' – a cold glint in their eyes.

Slowly, anger turned to stunned disbelief: not at the disappearance of the thief, but that they had allowed themselves to be taken in like that. Disbelief silently simmered into shame. For each, the revelation that they were rapacious was shameful. Gone now yesterday's boastfulness. Indeed, very few openly admitted to having taken part in the Push-Push scheme. And those, only when asked. The majority were plainly embarrassed and tight-lipped about the whole affair.

When they were sure no one could overhear them, men whose tongues had been loosened by drink would ask each other some of the hard questions swirling non-stop inside their heads.

'How could we begin to think such a thing could happen? And continue to happen? Till when? Where did we think all this manna came from? Why did we think anyone wise enough to make that kind of money would be foolish enough to give it away? And to people who were nothing at all to him?'

In many homes, husbands and wives blamed each other for the loss they had incurred. The number of couples separating or divorcing was so significantly higher than usual that year that people remarked: 'Is it not a plague that has come to Blouvlei? How come so many homes are breaking up all at once?' They were clearly disconcerted.

A man tried to drown himself in the Vlei, a stream to the north of Blouvlei and on the other side of which lay Boer farms.

One of the farmers found him submerged in water, semi-conscious, and stark naked. The Boer hauled him out of the water and proceeded to give him a sound thrashing. That quickly returned him to his senses. But in his haste to put distance between himself and the biting *sjambok*, he forgot his clothes where he had hidden them beneath a rock at the edge of the Vlei and ran all the way back to his house. A priest escaped being defrocked by the narrowest margin possible: one vote. He was given a year's suspension from duty without pay for the unauthorized use of church funds.

The aftermath of Push-Push was by no means confined to those who had been duped out of their money. Some of those who had received theirs back multiplied many times over, had their fair share of other sorts of troubles. Couples quarrelled over how their new-found wealth should be spent. Spouses found infidelity more intolerable than before – now that it went hand in glove with the family assets. People who had lent others money demanded a share of the profit and not just repayment of the loans. In short, few seemed to be better off for having taken part in Push-Push. And an old man lost his life because of the scheme.

Grandpa Goba was a very dignified man, much respected in the community, and very poor. He had three beautiful daughters, the eldest of whom was getting married. Her *ikhazi* was said to be over five hundred Rands, the husband-to-be was said to be both well-to-do and generous. Grandpa Goba put most of the money into Push-Push and was handsomely rewarded for his pains. He got almost five thousand some said. Others maintained that such a figure was a gross exaggeration. However, all agreed he did get a tidy sum. Everyone was looking forward to the wedding day; Blouvlei expected a feast fit for the wedding of a princess.

Shortly before the great day, the shack Grandpa Goba called home caught fire. The old man, told his house was on fire, ran back from minding his goats up on the hill. When he saw his house up in flames, Grandpa Goba cried out: 'My daughter's *ikhazi*! My poor child! How will I give her a wedding!' So saying, he threw himself into the fiery tongues. It happened so fast, before any could stop him he was already inside the furnace.

A hush fell. A stunned silence was disturbed only by the hissing juices of the wood and the crackling of zinc as the fire consumed the house. All eyes were on the burning shack; scouring the flames, searching for movement, the slightest sign, anything showing where hands might reach and pull; help get the old man out. But the greedy fire refused to yield its prey.

Hours later, when the fire had eventually died down, Grandpa Goba's frame was found hunched over the well-preserved shape of a box. Or rather what had been a box. Only, the box and the bundle of notes in it crumbled to the touch. They turned to dust; nothing but dust you could blow away with just your breath.

Following this episode, people said the Push-Push money was Satan's money. 'What good has it done even those who did get it?' they asked.

In my home, Father's lament at 'having been swayed by my wife's insistence,' was long and bitter whilst Mama never stopped reminding any who cared to listen; 'Were it not for Slow Coach, we would want for nothing today.' And, when particularly vexed, she'd add, 'And whose money was it, anyway, that we put in the bank, mmhh? So, whose money d'you think the bank gave him when he got that loan?'

Eventually though, the topic was laid to rest.

Years later, when I don't know what brought it to my mind and I asked my parents, 'By the way, how much did you two put into the Push-Push thing?' I was greeted with a stony silence. And then, as if trying hard to remember some remote event of little significance, Mama scrunched her now wrinkled face and asked, 'My, what makes you remember that, Nozimbo? You were, let's see ... how old were you? Three? Four?'

'I was already in school, Mama!'

'Oh, yes. Yes, that's right, you were. That was so long ago, how can you remember any of that?' She looked at my father, looked him straight in the eye and asked: 'Papa, do you recall that foolishness that cost half of the people here their money?' And Father replied, 'Serves them right too, I said then and I will say it now. Serves them damn right!'

Comrade, Heal Yourself!

From the baby-soft feel of the touch of his hand, the velvety sheen of the skin of his face, to the perfect match of what he wore, luxurious silks and soft, lush wools – each garment quietly announcing DESIGNER – the young man oozed the self-contained confidence of those who know there's no question of their ever going without, people to whom meals are a taken-for-granted matter of fact, as air to birds.

His morning had started at six o'clock. After he'd flipped through the newspapers, he'd got up and gone for a good jog. It being a Sunday, he went the long route – one whole hour instead of the half an hour with which he had to content himself during the week, including Saturdays, when he took his wife shopping. He'd made good time too and had even managed forty laps in the swimming pool. Having showered and changed, he went to join his wife for breakfast. She, nine months pregnant, no longer accompanied him on his morning fitness sessions. The couple sat in the upstairs veranda just off their bedroom and waited for the servant to bring breakfast. Madam had already given instructions.

Hearing him approach, she asked, 'Had fun?' and poured him a glass of orange juice.

'Uh–huh!' he mumbled, still tingling from the swim. 'But I can't wait for the day you'll run with me again.' He smiled right into her eyes and brushed his lips against her upturned cheek.

'D'you think I'll ever be able to run again?'

'Of course, silly! In no time at all you'll be out and about.'

Dubiously, the other looked at him. A slow smile crinkled the outer corners of her eyes. 'I feel like a veritable elephant, right now. I can hardly lift an arm.' She demonstrated as, with much show and exaggeration, she pushed one arm up; cupping the elbow in the hand of its opposite, grunting and groaning, she heaved upwards whilst making the arm heavy from the shoulder down. 'You see what I mean?' And they both burst out laughing. Just then, the servant, bringing in a heavily–laden tray, brought the hilarity to an abrupt stop.

Masondo watched his wife as she filled his plate with exactly the right mix of cereal: just so much Muesli with a spoon or so of two of the others – Corn Flakes, Rice Crispies, or Raisin Bran; doing that without once asking him how much of what he wanted. He felt the familiar cold clutch his heart. He felt his heart contract. For the zillionth time, he wondered whether he would ever get used to the idea of his singular good fortune – to be married to Sisipho, a woman who combined exquisite beauty with such a fine brain and then, as though that were not blessing enough, had such vitality and drive; good-hearted to boot. Man! Once again, he thanked his lucky stars that he had chosen the scholarship to NYU. He shuddered to think what would have happened if he had opted for Berkeley. Thanks to his shyness of earth-quakes, he had chosen the east coast despite its extremes of cold and heat. And it is this that led him to his bliss. Sisipho was also in New York although at a different university. The two had met at a South African New Year's Party. It was love at first sight for both of them, as they were to discover later when they shared the impact of that first encounter. What she saw in him, was still a mystery to Masondo. Early on in the evening, his eyes had been drawn irresistibly to the tall beauty with the figure of a goddess, caramel skin and lashes so long, even when they looked straight ahead, the slanted eyes appeared closed. Oh, yes, he'd definitely liked what he saw. He'd manoeuvred his way near her.

They had been married for more than two years now although to Masondo the relationship still felt a brand new wonder of only yesterday. Such was the sweetness in their life.

'Dearie, we'll be late for Mass,' he helped her up and they went inside. Moments later, he went to get the car from the garage while she put finishing touches to her toilette.

By the time they returned from Church, lunch was ready. On Sundays, his surgery hours were two to seven-thirty; he would be off soon. Bed for her. Her gynaecologist had ordered rest. Lots of rest. Her feet had taken to swelling in the last two weeks.

'I want you to rest now,' the husband said, hovering over his wife like an anxious mother hen. 'Otherwise we won't go out tonight,' he threatened, trying very hard to look stern. But his lips quivered suspiciously, betraying him.

Going along with his play, she made a sorry-looking face; eyes widening in disbelief. 'Not go to my own sister's birth-day party?' The querulous voice paused as though the speaker were baffled. Then it exploded – 'You tyrant! You can't stop me. And you know, Maud would kill us. Besides, there's no law that says ...'

'Yes, there is! Any action that poses a risk to my baby, is henceforth forbidden! Until you regain your former figure, you are remanded to your bed and will receive a hundred kisses an hour, by telephone, if necessary. Any questions?'

'Your Honour, I must appeal.'

'Woman, you may not trifle with this court!'

'But, Your Honour ...'

'No buts.' Taking her in his arms, he slowly waltzed back-wards and thus drew her gently to bed. Lips locked in tender kiss, he lay her down and sat beside her.

'*Bhabha*, pity I have to go to work.' His voice a little husky, again he kissed her slowly and leisurely. Then, abruptly, he released her. They were both breathing hard and fast.

'Woman,' he admonished, 'you will be my undoing yet! I am about to be a father, you know? What do you think this baby is going to eat? He has to go to school too, remember?'

'I knew it! I knew it!' screamed Sisipho, tears of laughter streaming down her cheeks. 'Already, I am second best, and this child not even born yet! What is to become of me after she has come?'

'Let me run to work, Baby. One of us has to be responsible,' Mosondo said, looking at her solemnly. His gaze lingered long on Sisipho's face before he added, almost as an afterthought, 'Know what? ... Until death do us part, my love, you will always be number one in my heart. This young man will leave me one day, he'll find his own sweetness somewhere I dare say. But you and I, you and I, we will be together till the end of time.'

'Till the end of time, darling.' She gave him an impish smile and cried out, 'But, it's a young woman we've ordered, sweetheart, not a young man!'

'Why don't we go for an ultrasound?'

'Because, I don't want to know. I want it to be a surprise.'

'But why? Why not take advantage of modern technology?'

'Ever heard the saying: Too much know sometimes bad?'

'Yes, but there is another saying ...'

'Darling, just call me old-fashioned; but I really enjoy the anticipation ... I appreciate the very absence of concrete evidence or, should I say, definite, conclusive fact? Can you understand that, Doctor?'

'You're right. We'll wait.' Rapidly, he nodded his head several times then, once more, added, 'You are right.' In a gesture of defeat, he drew his shoulders up to his ears, arms hanging loosely to his side, palms out, head bowed.

'Aha! Why does that remind me of something we said

when we first met?' said a giggling Sisipho.

'Correction! Something *you* said, Honey. You know now that foolishness certainly didn't come from my mouth.'

Eventually, after more teasing and kissing, 'making up', Masondo finally tore himself away from his beloved. At the door he turned, winked and blew her a kiss.

She saw him as though he were in a photograph: standing there, framed by the door, sunlight and sky way behind him, far beyond the veranda. Her heart welled with love. 'I LOVE YOU,' silently, she mouthed the words.

Floating on happiness, he waved a cheery goodbye. And left.

For the briefest of moments, she held the picture of him standing by the doorway in her mind's eye. And then the gap he had left intruded and blotted him out. With a sigh, she fell back onto her pillow and closed her eyes.

The time was a quarter before the hour.

Fifteen minutes later, the jet-black, gleaming Mercedes Benz 220 C glided to a silent stop in front of the doctor's surgery at the corner of NY 1 and NY 50, Guguletu. Masondo stepped out. His eye flew west to the mountain. It never stopped to amuse him that now that he had moved up in the world and had a house in Newlands he no longer enjoyed the splendid view of Table Mountain that had been his for the taking all his life while he lived in the squalor of the township.

He strode towards the surgery. 'Good–afternoon, dear,' he greeted the nurse who met him at the door. As they made their way through the waiting-room, he nodded left and right to his patients. In return, he was greeted with murmurs of satisfaction and grunts of 'Afternoon, Doctor,' and there was much shuffling as they began to rearrange themselves into order according to the well–known 'First Come, Front Seated' law of doctors' waiting-rooms the world over. The doctor noted with a measure of gratification that there was a sizeable crowd. Things had changed. Unlike the one-or-no-doctor situation of his childhood, these days, although no one could say the African townships suffered a surfeit of medical doctors, enough of them had come to generate mild competition. And not only African doctors either. There was a healthy sprinkling of Indian, Coloured, and even white doctors in LAGUNYA these days. And a good thing too, Masondo believed.

Sundays were his busiest days. People were paid on Fridays but worked Saturdays. So, Sunday was the first and only day they were both free and still had money in their pockets.

The nurse had been with him for almost a year. Right at that moment, she was busy with her end-of-year exams. She attended night school at St Francis Adult Education Centre in Langa. A must, for anyone who worked for him. She was his second nurse. The first young woman who'd worked for him was now at Livingstone Hospital in Port Elizabeth, in her second year there, training to be a nurse. He'd coaxed her into completing her high-school education too. Nomfundo, the present nurse, would follow that route, unless she chose to do something else once she got her matric. It was up to her what course of study she would undertake. What wasn't, what he absolutely insisted on, was that no one in his employ park herself there for ever. Waste of time. Squandering of lives.

That is what had happened to his mother. A bright woman. A hard worker. She had worked all her life as Doctor Shaffer's 'nurse'. When she'd been younger, she had fallen pregnant in her third year as a trainee nurse at King Edward VIII Hospital in Durban. Expelled and too ashamed and too scared to go back to her family in Umtata, she had fled to Cape Town, where she ended up working for the Indian doctor.

Furthering one's studies was one of the few stipulations he

made to anyone he was considering hiring. On that, he absolutely insisted. Two years, three at the very most, was all the time any woman, or man, was going to spend in his surgery. He'd watched his mother's deterioration. She began to dip into the doctor's supply; on the sly, sell dermatological products she stole from the surgery; give people injections at her home; again, stuff she'd taken without the doctor's knowledge. Inevitably, that's what happens when people are trapped in dead-end jobs, however glamorous those may be. Expectations eventually outstrip income. And there is the gross lack of stimulation, the blurring of vision that comes with the tedious repetition of tasks long learnt and stubbornly unchanging. No, his practice would never become another human being's death trap. No one working for him would wake up after twenty years and look back only to realize that all they had ever done in that time was to call out: Next! to patients with a sickeningly unvarying list of diseases; dispense medicine he'd prescribed, explain the same instructions over and over again: *two full tablespoons, four times a day – two teaspoonfuls, four times a day – with meals … Three tablets …* No. Not if he had any say in the matter. And, he did.

Nomfundo was a fast learner with a good head on her shoulders; calm in an emergency, unflappable. He was quite pleased with her work and today was no exception. The two soon fell into an easy rhythm and the hours sped swiftly by, without a hitch.

Six forty-five. His heart gladdened at the thinning numbers, which he noticed when, as he often did, he talked to a patient right to the surgery door, leading out to the waiting-room. Now, his casual glance told him: Less than ten. Barring emergencies, they should finish on time. He'd hate to keep Sisipho waiting; she was quite excited about tonight. Although he was a little tired, he knew the outing would do both of them a world of good. He enjoyed night life.

However, he planned to be in bed by midnight. And that was possible, if he closed on time. The earlier they went to the party, the earlier they could excuse themselves. Maud would be the first to urge them to go home. She was solicitous of her youngest sister, particularly now, with the baby expected in a matter of days.

From her little corner of the waiting-room, Nomfundo surveyed the room. With satisfaction, she too noticed the numbers had dwindled; it was almost time to go home, she mused. She was going over her log book when something made her look at the remaining patients again. Her right wrist resting slightly on the open page, the hand fell on its back in slight puzzlement, lifting the pen off the page in mid word.

'*He, Mdlezana,*' she called out to the young mother, one of only three people still waiting, and asked her, 'What have you done with the three patients who were sitting next to you?'

'*Hayi, Nesi!*' said the poor woman in confusion. '*Andikhange ndibenze nto. Basuke baziphumela.* I didn't do anything to them. They just went out.'

Nomfundo laughed; told the other not to be such a coward. Seeing a look of consternation on her face, Nomfundo told her she had only been joking. 'They are big, grown–up men, and can certainly take care of themselves.' The baby's mother smiled her relief.

Fifteen minutes before closing, with only the baby's mother waiting, the doctor still busy with another patient, the three men returned. Perhaps they'd gone outside because of the No Smoking signs, Nomfundo told herself. Nonetheless, she was annoyed with them.

'We're about to close, now.' Her voice was shrill to her own ears. I must exercise better control, she cautioned herself. But she couldn't quite quell her anger at them. Where did they think they were, toing and froing like this? She'd already told the doctor that the next patient would be his last for the evening.

'We came back just in time then, my sister!' said one, all his front teeth missing. *Fishgap*, Nomfundo immediately labelled him.

She was still thinking of an appropriate retort … my sister, indeed! when *Fishgap* went on, 'You see, we …'

Too much. She wasn't going to stand there the whole night listening to the imbecile; oh no. 'Okay, wait here. I'll see if the doctor will take one more.' Just before she reached the door, Nomfundo stopped, turned around, 'By the way,' she said, 'which one of you is here to see him?'

'All of us,' came the improbable reply from one of *Fishgap*'s companions, a rather stout fellow. *Fishgap* himself grunted his support of the squab's statement. Nomfundo's eyes flew wide open, taken aback by the asinine response. The third man must have seen she was annoyed. He hastily amended:

'That is not true, Nurse. *I* have come to see the doctor. My friends here, they're just jokers. Please disregard what they say. But they are good men, Nurse. Good men. See how they've stayed with me all this time? They want to make sure I do the right thing.'

Startled by his back-massaging baritone, Nomfundo frantically fought to maintain a cool she was far from feeling. Nodding her head, she beat a rather inelegant retreat into the safety of the doctor's consultation room; the baby's mother, whom she had beckoned, trailing her.

'I'm terribly sorry, doctor, but after this one, there's one more still, I'm afraid. He'd been here earlier.'

'That's okay,' replied Masondo, his eye already on the new patient, an infant. 'Less than six months,' judged the doctor, looking at the size of the bundle; amused too at how carefully, like a basket of newly-laid eggs, the young mother carried it. To Nomfundo, he said, 'By the way, you may leave, now. I'll take care of the next one ... and I'll close. I'll see to everything ... you go.'

'Thank you, doctor. But, are you sure?' She knew he was letting her leave early because she was writing exams. But had he not said he and his wife were going out? He could use the help in closing if he were rushing somewhere ...

But the doctor, seeing her hesitate, said, 'Good-night. Go ahead now. Go and swot. I'll see you tomorrow.'

'The doctor will see you when the patient he's seeing comes out, okay?'

'Ta, my sister.'

There was something Nomfundo did not like about these men. Too familiar, for one thing. *Fishgap* and his *puza face*. *My sister*! She was fuming but saw that there was no time to be squabbling with them. What would it help, anyway?

She had already tidied up. Now, she took off her flat, lace-up shoes and put on a black pair of mid–heeled pumps, grabbed her bag, and left; closing the door softly behind her as she did.

A few minutes after the baby and her mother had left Masondo called in his last patient. 'You may come in!' – he shouted, furiously scribbling into the note pad he kept in his pocket. When he looked up, he was surprised at seeing three men crowded just inside the door.

'What can I do for you, gentlemen?' He walked towards the door, thinking – what have we got here? ... A reluctant patient, who's had to be dragged here most likely. But the response he got threw him.

'We have come to see you.' And that was more than just one voice.

'You want to see me? All three of you?' He did not know what had led him to ask such an unnecessary question. Impractical, anyway. How could he possibly see all three at once? And he certainly didn't have time to see more than one more patient tonight ... even that was pushing it a bit, as it were. He glanced at his watch.

'You could say that, Doctor.' Why did he detect sarcasm in the man's voice?

'But ... which one has come to see me? Who is the sick one?'

'We are all sick, Doctor ... all of us.' Someone laughed. At least, that was what Masondo chose to call the sound, grating; devoid of mirth.

Now, he looked at the men, paying attention. Their stance was confrontational. Unless he was imagining things. But no ... the way they stood ... something in the raucous cackle ... in the ensuing silence...*Quick!* his mind told him, *think of something* ...

A hold up! Panic and confusion whirled in his head. 'Why don't you wait back out there.' With authority, he ushered them out of the door. Pointing towards the long, silent benches he said, 'Let me complete the last patient's entry.' He hurried inside, closing the screen door. How he wished he had a real door there now – one he could lock. He reached for the phone.

Dead.

How had that happened? Frantically, his fingers jabbed at the phone buttons. Again and again. Disbelief mounting.

'That's no use!' came a cool voice from the doorway. All his focus on raising the alarm, Masondo had not heard the screen being pushed open. The man at the door regarded him with amused hostility; belligerent.

'We cut it from in here, doctor,' said the walking brewer's vat, as he gestured in the general direction of the nurse's table. The face repulsed Masondo, who was amazed at how at ease and unhurried the intruder appeared.

'What do you want?' And, without thinking, he made for the chair where his patients sat as he talked to them. But

Fishgap jerked his head, indicating that he should go to the outer room. Masondo hesitated ... shrugged his shoulders, and walked through the door, past the toothless one and into the waiting-room. The man followed him out.

Masondo now turned his attention to the other men. They had preceded him to the far side of the room and were seated on the benches there. A remarkable duo, one so fair he looked coloured, the other black as a *mphokoqo* pot. And lubberly as hell. All this, Masondo took in at once – looking at them sitting there, their necks and bare hands giving him these clues. Only now did he realize that all three were virtually masked; wearing wollen skull caps and goggles.

'Gentlemen,' he fought to keep his voice reasonable, as though this were an ordinary, everyday conversation. 'We are about to close. What can I do for you?' He must take charge somehow, he reminded himself.

'*Ja*, Doc!' said Blackie.

Masondo stood there, looking at them, trying to figure out his next move, trying to still the bats crazily flapping around in mad panic in his stomach.

Without looking at it, the man who had come into the surgery dragged the nurse's chair, sent it scuttling across the floor towards him. Unlike the other two, he didn't have a jacket on. His arms were long and sinewy. Masondo caught the chair, but remained standing.

'Sit!' barked *Fishgap*, while he himself remained standing and slightly kitty–corner to his mates on the bench. Masondo noted that the man stood blocking the door to the street. Had they locked it? What would they do if someone came looking for him?

Nomfundo. If only he had not let Nomfundo go. But then, she was preparing for exams. How could he have kept her late. That would have been selfish in the extreme ... not when he didn't really need her. Oh, why didn't someone come ... a late patient ... an emergency ... or a friend passing by ... just checking to see if he was still in ... why didn't someone knock at the door! His eyes bored holes through the door; surely, God would send someone, now?

'Go see that the door is locked.'

The growl came from the man Masondo was sure was from Mannenberg or another of the coloured townships. His Xhosa, though, told him now, 'Forget that!' No six months 'Let us Learn Xhosa' course would ever produce that inflection of voice. At once, *Gargantua* ran to the door.

'It is locked,' he reported. Masondo felt his heart turn to ice. His last hope was dashed.

'Then switch the lights off. We don't want our chat here with the good doctor interrupted.' Again that was the man from Mannenberg. This time, *Fishgap* responded to the order with alacrity.

They were not in total darkness, however. The surgery door ajar, there was enough light from that source for them to see without its attracting much attention from the street.

A heavy silence fell.

After a while, Masondo could not bear the suspense. He wanted to get to the bottom of this – see what's what and who's who.

'Yes, *Bajita*?' Keep calm, he interrupted his own thoughts. Obviously, they are not going to kill you. Give them what they want and let them go. The police will deal with them later on. Briefly, his mind wandered and he thought of his wife. She would worry. He'd last spoken to her at six – six-thirty. No, she wouldn't start worrying until after eight. Maybe he could still make it. Maybe he'd be back by then.

'*Broer*, there is something we don't understand. We thought maybe you could help us, so that is why we are here.'

He made a non-committal grunt that could pass for question or a simple yes.

'Do you remember us?' He looked hard at their faces, what

he could see of their faces, hidden beneath those heavy hats and sunglasses.

'No, I can't say that I do. I can't really see who you are ... your faces.' His mind darted here and there and everywhere else; dredging the murky waters of recent memory. Blank. He could think of no episode from which this confrontation could be arising.

'You really don't know us, do you?' The spokesman took off his hat. He took off his sunglasses. Masondo had a vague, very vague memory, dim, of a face once familiar ... a face from afar ... or from a long time ago. He dug the bottom of his brain, *blank*. Probably before his days of indulging, if I ever knew him, went his thoughts. Perhaps, when he still had all his teeth.

'You said I may be able to help you?' Might as well hear their story. These thugs probably wanted drugs. And here he was worrying himself about money. But whatever it was they were after, he should just give it to them, that was the only way he would rid himself of such vermin. Irritation fought to overthrow fear and anger. He had things to do. Caution. The word painted itself in his brain. Caution. Big and bright and red.

'*Broer*, you know, my friends and I,' Now the elephantine one took over. He paused and glanced towards his companions, one seated on the bench and the other, like himself, standing. They nodded and he continued. 'There's this little thing we want you to explain to us ... *How on earth does it happen that today you are a doctor?*' he said in a hard, harsh whisper.

Not that! His heart raced like a thing demented. A yawning abyss gaped before his eyes. Cold sweat slithered down his spine. His palms clammy, his throat quite parched, 'I don't understand,' he said. He did not recognize the voice that croaked through his dry, dry lips.

'Hey *Maa'n*, don't give us that *shit*, here.' Suddenly,

Fishgap bent down and brought his face so close to Masondo's, the latter could see the hairs inside his nostrils. His hand shot down towards Masondo's neck. A cold line drew itself with the sharpness of cold steel all around his throat. Masondo swallowed involuntarily.

'Hey! Let me tell you something, doctor. *We* are the fools who didn't go to school. What d'you mean you don't understand? *We* are the only idiots who can say that. *We* don't understand how you, a leader of the comrades, stands there today wearing a white overcoat.' Snarling, Blackie waddled over towards Masondo and came and planted his massive self next to *Fishgap*.

'Doesn't he look grand, *Bajita*?' – he asked; his eyes full of anger, hatred, and a murderous venom.

Next, there was a jab at his chest. Another knife? This time he had not seen it coming. Besides, the point of the first was still on his Adam's apple. He felt the sharp prick though. Probably not deep enough to break the skin ... perhaps a graze? Nothing that would draw blood, however. Which one had thrust it this time? How many knives did the thugs bring with them? More to the point, what were they after?

A gruff voice interrupted these thoughts.

'*Jaa*, he looks grand all right. And did you check his car?' That was *Fishgap*. The light–skinned one continued to hold his peace. He was a man of few and infrequent words, apparently. Masondo reverted to his earlier notion about him, perhaps he *was* coloured after all. Or was not really in total accord with what the other two were up to. The latter thought raised hope in Masondo's heart. He could appeal to him, the decent fellow!

But *Fishgap* was not yet done. 'Do you know he lives in the white areas? Even the chick he married, Maa'n, she too works with the *lannies*. She drives her own car, Maa'n. Bought it herself before they were married. They say she is a lawyer!'

'*Jaa*!' Blackie drew a long, sharp whistle that ended in a thin–blown tail: *Whoooeeeiieeee*. No one could doubt the mockery of his surprise. His eyebrows shot up and chased the hairline while his chin dropped and his mouth made an imperfect *0*. His eyes big as an owl's, 'The man is big!' boomed his voice.

'Ye-e-es! He sure is. And now, he's going to tell us how he got to where he is.' Glowering at Masondo, *Fishgap* growled, 'Aren't you, Doctor?'

An involuntary groan escaped from Masondo's mouth as red pain flashed through his back, somewhere below his right shoulder blade. He felt his knees yield. His left hand wound itself under the right armpit and snaked around to his back. There it met the slowly spreading warm sticky wet on his coat. Even as he fingered the slight swell of raw flesh beneath the coat, the pain subsided. But he knew it would come back.

'So, tell us! When did you go to school?'

He could feel cold gnaw his insides. Just as he opened his bone-dry mouth to answer the question, his mind telling him he was in one big heap of trouble, another question flew at him –

'Were you not one of the people going around with big signs and shouting "Down with Bantu Education!" and "Liberation first – Education later!" Heh?'

'Yes, *Bajita*. But later on I stopped boycotting.'

'Ooh! He stopped boycotting!' Again Blackie feigned surprise. 'Did you hear that?' he looked from the one to the other of his companions. 'He stopped boycotting.' His serpentine gaze returned to the doctor as he queried, 'But what happened to "Bantu Education cannot be reformed – It must be abolished!"?'

Masondo could not find words to respond to the tirade. Undeterred, the other continued:

'Now, *Mfowethu*, I don't remember anyone shouting to us,

telling us "Go back to school" or "Education now, Liberation later".' To the other two, a by-now quite agitated Blackie asked, 'Does either of you, my brothers?' And when they shook their heads in decline, he added wryly, 'Well, maybe we're deaf now. Deaf as well as stupid. Dumb. But, we weren't deaf then. In 1976 we listened to your words. Words you said. Words we heard.'

He took his knife and, drawing a line along the left side of Masondo's face – from temple to chin – through clenched teeth he hissed: 'Did you remember us when you were studying?' Hand firm on knife. Cutting.

A burning sensation shot through that side of Masondo's face. He flinched. His throat burned. His armpits warm and crawling, his head began to ache. He could think of nothing to say.

'*Awu*, Doc, you mean you don't appreciate us coming for a chat? We spend all this time waiting for you and now you will not talk to us?' Again a knife bit into his flesh ... the upper left arm, this time. They were not out to kill him ... but were sure inflicting enough damage. Masondo let out a scream ... only, it came out as a little startled yelp.

'It was my mother who ... She ... after we ...' he lost his trend of thought. The offer of the scholarship flashed before his eyes.

They'd take his special circumstances into account, New York University had informed him. He would be given a year's intense tutoring, all expenses paid, to make up for the two years of high school he had lost. How well he remembered the excitement. And the fear. He had wavered. Then his mother's words removed the dilemma: *They are your father or your mother? ... these children who are telling you not to go to school? How can you throw away such good fortune?* Now, those words rang in his ears, as clear as though she were in that room, as though it were that other day, long ago.

But a voice from the pressing present intruded on these private thoughts. It yanked him back to the awful reality of the minute.

'Let me make things easy for the doctor. *Mhlekazi*, now that we see you driving around in a *Msindisi*, you have a big house with a swimming pool ... a house in the white areas ... what ... about ... us?' The last three words came out in a long, low, drawn-out sneer. But, in them, Masondo saw a way out, a glimmer of hope. Faint. But there.

There was his chance. Maybe he could buy his way out of this. 'I don't have a lot of money here in the surgery, Gentlemen, maybe two thousand rand, that's all. But you can have all that.'

'Two thousand rands? What can we buy with two thousand rands? A car?'

'No, Gentlemen, that is just for tonight. Tomorrow, as soon as the banks open, I will give you more.'

'How much?'

'Twenty thousand.'

'Twenty, each?' The bag of lard was scowling in earnest concentration.

'Yes. Twenty to each man.'

Blackie was breathless. He turned to his friends, 'Did you hear that?' he asked. The others remained silent.

'What do you think? Shall we accept his offer?' Again Blackie asked. The hand holding the knife hung loosely to his side.

'It seems pretty good to me,' *Fishgap* responded, eyes bright.

'No!' Slowly, Blackie shook his head. He looked sad. Apparently, he'd had a rethink. His voice rising, he went on, 'What happens when we've spent that money? You see, he got himself an education. He can give us twenty thousand rands each tomorrow. In a month, that's all gone. You buy a car, a few suits to go with the car, a leather coat. Give some to your mother. Treat your lady to something nice. You can't be seen around with a chick whose clothes look like they came from the church rummage sale now, can you? After all that, where d'you get the money to run the car? A car needs petrol. A car has worse *bhabhalaza* than the biggest drunk you know. Cars are always thirsty and refuse to budge if you don't give them a drink.'

'*Jaa*!' Enjoined Fishgap, 'Cars are the worst guzzlers,' several times, his head went slowly up and down as though he were figuring out the solution to a particularly difficult puzzle.

'No, *Bajita*,' said Blackie, 'it won't work.' There was genuine regret in his voice as he answered his own rhetoric.

His heart sank right down to the blocks of ice that used to be his ankles. *What* did they want. 'I can arrange for you to get more. But you would have to give me a little time to raise the loan.'

'Shut up!' The voice whipped the air. A new voice. Now, it continued, 'You still don't understand, do you?' And he saw the other two thugs shiver and appear to shrink at just the sound of the voice. The fair-skinned one had spoken at last.

'Doc! Doc! Doc!' He looked at Masondo as, pityingly, he slowly shook his head. 'It's not your money we want, Doc … or, should I say, *Comrade*?' His speech was unhurried. His voice though, full–bodied. 'You didn't take money from us. You went back to school … after telling us to stop going to school. Today, we are nothing; *you* are a doctor. We will never have money or the good life. *You*, live in luxury. What d'you think about that?'

'It was not my fault, Gentlemen. I was a child. Others told us what to do. Like you, I was told what to do, what to say.'

'But, somehow, *Comrade*,' no sharper knife could pierce his heart, Masondo found; '*you* managed to find your way back to school.'

The mildly accusing tone of the past few minutes was gone.

There was a new quality in the voice. Chilling. Menacing. Now, sweat poured down the doctor's spine. Or, was that his blood?

He thought of the nurse. The surgery had no window. It was to the back of the building, away from the street ... to avoid noise. No. He could not hope for help from that source. Maybe his wife. Sisipho might call. Would she get suspicious when, after several attempts, she couldn't raise him? Hardly, given the appalling telephone service in the townships. Also, she might take it he was on his way and had forgotten to call her to tell her that ... or, he'd been pressed for time. It had happened before ... No, she would only get concerned hours later, if he did not show up ... and there was no word from him, saying there was this or that emergency. He must ... play for time.

'Could I have some water, please?' He was feeling a bit faint. His feet were sticky in his shoes, some liquid had got into the shoes ...

'My big problem is', the same chilly voice continued; it was a frightening voice – low, soft, and deliberate, 'my problem is, *Comrade-doctor*, I do not recall your words telling us it was okay to go back to school.' Each word was enunciated with cold, careful clarity. 'And now, we are too old. Our chances are gone. Gone! Full stop!'

Suddenly, the voice rose, filled with an unspeakable rage. Agitated, the speaker, now on his feet, strode about the room.'

'Do you hear me, Dog? Our chances are gone. GONE! Dog! They are gone! Forever lost!'

This man was the most dangerous of the lot! The thought struck Masondo numb. He realized then that he had pinned too much hope on his presence, seeing in it a mediating factor. A gross error of judgement on his part: while the first two men might hurt him, this man was deadly. I must do something! Must pacify them! Stifling rising panic, palpable as the furniture in the room, he told himself: Whatever it is that I have to do, I'd better do it fast. Otherwise, I'm dead meat.

'What can I do for you now, *Manene?*' The irony hit him. This was one of the first questions he'd asked them at the very beginning. In all this time, they had but travelled the short distance of a pin point, a dot. He still did not have a way out. Now, of course, he knew a whole lot more about what he was faced with. He found himself on his feet; hands clasped in supplication. He had not felt himself get up from the chair. Now, a wild urge to throw himself at the feet of these three men overcame him. He wanted to go on his knees, beg their forgiveness. His eye darted to their pockets. For the first time since the whole nightmare began, he knew, with absolute certainty, that his life meant nothing at all to them. They would kill him with as much compassion and conscience as if they were squashing a bed bug.

As though to confirm Masondo's fears, the last speaker walked right up to him and gave him a sound kick in the groin. Masondo doubled over. That was an invitation for his assailant, this man whose silence earlier on had led him to think he might be the means to his salvation, to go to town.

He no longer knew which of the three was attacking him.

'What do you want, now?' The calm strength of his voice surprised him. It infuriated the quiet one, he of fair skin. He drew out an ugly-looking gun and, pointing it at Masondo, yelled:

'Boys! Did you hear that? He wants to know what we want.' Then turning to Masondo, he spat out: 'There's something I want you to understand, *comrade*. This is not just about the three of us. But it is for all the millions of us – children then – whom you and people like you aborted, *enabaqhomfayo!* ... Now, *comrade*, do you understand?'

Having delivered his sermon, the man stepped back. 'He's all yours!' he said; letting go of Masondo, who crumpled in a heap on the floor.

In a frenzy, the other two fell on the already bleeding man with their daggers. Very soon, he couldn't feel the blows.

'That's enough!' rang the order. 'Let's get out of here,' barked the fair-skinned one. He still held the gun and had not participated in the knifing. His were the only hands not stained red.

Masondo never saw him approach. He didn't see him aim the gun at his head. His eyes were swollen shut. For a brief moment, the other stood poised above him, looking down; a bitter-sweet memory flashed through his mind.

Standard Six. 1971. June Exams. He'd lost his first position to this man. One mark. But, that had been the telling difference.

The finger tightened around the trigger. 'Heal yourself, *Comrade*, he said.

Masondo never heard the sound. There was none to hear, just a small soft plop; less than when the cork flies off a bottle of ginger beer. He didn't hear the words either. A bright light infused his whole body; brilliant as a mid–summer's dawn. He caught a fleeting glimpse of Sisipho, a chubby little fellow on her lap. His mother stood behind them, her face bathed in a dazzling smile.

Sisipho waited till well after eight before she called the surgery. Again she called ten minutes later. And again the line was dead. At eight-thirty, she called her sister. 'We are running late, I'm afraid,' she said. 'But we will be over as soon as he gets here.' She didn't like the excuse she was giving. People, including her own family, had an attitude about doctors and their perennial scheduling problems. She had long been ready.

Half an hour later, she called Nomfundo.

Nomfundo's reaction so alarmed Sisipho she again phoned

her sister's house and relayed the news. Soyiso, Maud's husband, assured her he would go over to the surgery and call her back as soon as possible. Taking a friend with him, he went via Nomfundo's home. She'd agreed to go with them as she had a key to the surgery, in case it was locked. Also, Masondo might have left a message or some other sign, something, anything, to explain the delay in getting home. More than anyone else, Nomfundo would be better able to tell.

Face up on the floor, in a pool of blood that had already started to congeal, lay Masondo. Except for Nomfundo's chair, which was not in its accustomed place, nothing else appeared disturbed. The office had not been ransacked, not even the desk drawers. The day's takings were still intact. Robbery, clearly, was not the motive in this killing.

Within minutes, the police were on the scene. And that is when the note was found.

THIS DOG IS A SELLOUT DO NOT GO TO HIS FUNERAL DO NOT GO TO THE FUNERAL OF A SELL-OUT WE WILL GET YOU TOO IF YOU DO EVEN IF YOU ARE A MINISTER YOU MUST NOT BURY THE SELLOUT

Masondo had died from a single bullet wound. Straight through the head.

The people of Guguletu were sufficiently intimidated for only immediate family to go to the wake of Doctor Masondo Masoka. And those who went didn't tarry long. Certainly, none stayed for the whole evening. And none came every evening. Therefore, most of the time the mother was there all alone. Unheard of among Africans, for one to be alone at a time of loss. A few, feeling relatively safe because they lived in the erstwhile white suburbs, took the risk of coming to the wake. But even those stopped by in the early evening and for only a few minutes. They had escaped the township and its endemic violence, had they not? Why then would they go and spend time there now? But that is where the wake was held. At his mother's home. Sisipho was in hospital. The shock had induced labour the same evening Masondo died, and she could not even attend the funeral.

All who heard of the episode were dismayed, but they were not that saddened that they would stick their necks out. Times had truly changed.

Each and every minister approached by the family found he was already booked for the Saturday, and for several following ones. And when the family changed the funeral service from Saturday to Sunday, most ministers had weddings, baptismals, and pressing family matters to see to – for a whole long month of Sundays to come.

Of the murder, the residents of Guguletu spoke in furtive tones. None wanted it said they were sympathetic to the murdered man or his family. Shaking heads, they whispered – Did you hear how this young, brilliant doctor was killed here in Guguletu? And did you hear how the grief-stricken woman, his mother, said only one thing when she was told of what had happened to her son? Only one thing: 'At least, they didn't burn him. I am luckier than some. I have a body to bury. My son was not necklaced.'

Yes, that is all Masondo's mother said. Those are the words she scooped out of her bleeding heart and used as a handkerchief to wipe the sorrow off her face.

It took time and a lot of doing, but at last, a minister from *The Zion in Afrika Church of Christ* came forward and offered his services, if the family would have him. The family was desperate. They were more than glad to use his services, they said.

That Saturday, a day short of two weeks after he was murdered by three young men whom the police had not yet apprehended, Masondo was laid to rest.

To be fair, the police had very little to go by. All Nomfundo could tell them was that she had last seen the deceased with three African men – or perhaps two Africans and one coloured man. She had not seen their faces nor could she recall any other detail about them – except that one of them had a remarkably rich baritone, like a singer's. None of the businessmen and businesswomen in the shopping complex had heard the report from the gun. Not even the shoemaker, right next to the surgery. This led the authorities to conclude that the killers had used a silencer.

The police investigation was not expected to be swift. It was not expected to yield results. During those times of an abundant harvest, none of the bloodthirsty reapers were ever brought to justice. To the white authorities, Masondo's murder was just one more of the typical acts of an inscrutable race.

The funeral itself was grim, brief, and purely functional. A lone car, bringing the minister and two neighbours, followed the hearse from the house to the graveyard, where, at the gate, two police vans stood watch. The minister performed the most abridged interment version ever witnessed in Guguletu.

The coffin had been lowered, soil thrown over it, and the two or three relatives were going back to the vehicles to return to the homestead and wash their hands as custom demanded. Suddenly, a group of young men and women appeared and surrounded the mourners, who were not armed. Even the police were caught with their pants down. Frantically, they radioed for reinforcements.

Fortunately, those who *toi-toied* around the bereaved had decided to be reasonable, to be lenient. Firing warning shots into the air, they gave their orders, directed primarily to the Man of God.

'*Mfundisi*, we give you half an hour to clear out of Cape Town. Half an hour. Try us, and see if we mean business or not! The time now is half past five,' they declared. 'See what happens to you if you're still anywhere around Cape Town by six!'

Shaken, Reverend Nongwe got into his car. He had a little trouble starting it, his hands were trembling so. Clutch grinding, he soon sped off, though. As he reached the gate, out of the *toi-toiing* crowd, rang a message, clear as a bell: 'More of us are waiting for you at your house! Your house is surrounded!'

The minister thought of his responsibility. When he had volunteered to bury this man, he'd known he was taking a risky step. But, he had a responsibility to his God, and to his fellowmen.

Those who were watching him, were amazed to see him drive down NY 108 and make not a turn, left or right, upon reaching NY 1. Instead, he continued straight on, crossed NY 1 and sped on along NY 108 and clear out of Guguletu. In less than five minutes flat! The minister had remembered his duty to his family.

Two days later, the good man of God phoned his wife. He was in Cofimvaba, he told her. She should pack everything and prepare for a move. Yes, he had already contacted the higher-ups in his church. Yes, it was agreed; he'd been due for a transfer, anyway. 'And, you know,' there was a slight pause, then the minister reminded her, 'I've always dreamt of working in a small village parish.'

I'm Not Talking
About That, Now

Mamvulane lay very still, her eyes wide open; staring unseeingly into nowhere. She listened to her husband snore softly besides her.

A big bold orange band lay on the carpet – painted there by the strong dawn light pouring through the bright orange-curtained window.

Reluctantly, she focused her eyes. Her head was throbbing. She glanced at the alarm clock on the dressing-table. God, it wasn't even five o'clock yet. How was she going to survive this day? she asked herself. Her right eye felt as though someone was poking a red-hot iron rod into it from the back of her head, where he'd first drilled a hole.

Irritatedly, she pushed her husband onto his side. Immediately, the snoring stopped. She listened to the drilling inside her head, assuming that with the noise of Mdlangathi's snoring gone, the pain would subside. And, indeed, it did appear to be in abeyance if not completely vanished.

She took a deep and noisy inward draw of breath. Cruel fancy played her tricks. She could swear the air was faintly laced with the barest soupçon of the bitter-sweet smell of coffee. Mmmhh! What she wouldn't give for just one cup. Just one.

Her stomach growled. Swiftly, she placed one hand on her still girlishly flat tummy. She felt the quick ripples of air bubbles in her bowels. When last had she eaten? And what had she had then?

Mdlangathi, her husband lying next to her, mumbled something in his sleep and turned over to lie, once more, facing the ceiling; his distinctly discernible paunch hilling the blankets.

Immediately, the snoring resumed; provoking swift and righteous retaliation from his wife; reflex by now, after all the years with him and his snoring.

Mamvulane dug an elbow into his side, grumbling, '*Uyarhona, Mdlangathi. Uyarhona!*' for habits die hard. In their more than twenty years of marriage, among the constants in their relationship was his snoring whenever he lay 'like a rat suffering from acute heartburn', her talking to him as though he were awake and the answers he never failed to mumble – pearls from an ancient oracle. She always chided herself that she actually listened, paid attention to the barely audible ramblings of a snoring man who'd gone to bed drunk. But she always did. And tonight, not only was he drunk when he went to bed, Mamvulane told herself, but she had never seen him so agitated. Would she never learn?

Last night, however, was the worst she'd ever seen him. He'd returned positively excited, ranting and raving about the gross lack of respect of today's young people.

'*Baqalekisiwe, ndifung' uTat' ekobandayo. Baqalekisiw' aba bantwana, Mamvulane.*'

'What children are cursed?' His wife wanted to know.

And that is when he told her of the curse the actions of today's children would surely invite onto their heads.

'Why do you say such a terrible thing?' his wife wanted to know.

'Now-now, just as the sun set, I was on my way here from the single men's zones, where I'd gone to get a little something to wet my parched throat. What do you think I should come across? Mmhhmh?' He stopped and considered the other with his bleary eyes.

His wife conceded ignorance. 'I'm sure I don't know. Why don't you tell me,' she said. She wanted to scrape together what food there was in the house. And try to prepare a meal.

'D'you know that a group of boys accosted a man? A grown man, who was circumcized? Boys laid their filthy hands on such a man ... a man old enough to be their father?'

'Where was this?' asked Mamvulane, not sure how much of Mdlangathi's ramblings she should take seriously.

'You ask me something I have already told you. Where are your ears, woman? Or else, you think I'm drunk and pay no attention to what I tell you? No wonder your children are as bad as they are, where would they learn to listen and obey since you, our wives, who are their mothers, have stopped doing that? Mmhhh?'

'Are you telling me the story or should I go about my business?' retorted Mamvulane. She was taking a risk, for she did want to hear the story. But she also knew that her husband rather fancied the sound of his own voice.

'If you want to hear the story, then pay attention. I told you I was from the zones. On my way here, I came across a group of boys, you know, these little rascals who are always passing by here, pretending to be visiting your son, Mteteli, when you full know it's your daughter they want. And they were manhandling one of their fathers.'

'Who was that?'

'Now, you make me laugh. You imagine I stopped and asked them for their *dompasses*? Am I mad? Or, do you think I am a fool? Or is it your hurry to be a widow that is putting those stupid words into your mouth? Mmhh?'

With great deliberateness, Mdlangathi attended to the business of picking his teeth. First, he took out a match. Then he took out his jack-knife and started whittling slowly on the tiny match, chiselling it till the back had a sharp point.

'When a woman told me what those dogs were doing, I

knew enough to mind my own business, my friend. Today's
children show no respect for their fathers.

'This man, the woman said to me, had had too much to
drink. Now, mind you,' quickly, he went to the defence of his
fallen comrade. '... the man drank from his own pocket, he
didn't ask those silly boys to buy him his liquor. So, what is
his sin? Tell me, what is this man's sin when he has drunk
liquor he bought with his own money? Why should these
mad children make that their business, mmhhmh?'

'What did they do?'

'These little devils,' bellowed Mdlangathi, eyes flashing,
'Don't they force the sad man to drink down a solution of
Javel? *Javel*, Mamvulane! Do you hear me? What do you
think *Javel* does to a man's throat? To his stomach? I ask
you, what do you think it does to those things? Just visit and
make jokes with them, heh?'

He glowered at her as though she were one of the 'little
devils' and he was itching to teach her a lesson.

Bang! went his fist on the table.

'A grown man, no less! The boys make him drink that poison. They tell him, 'We are helping you, Tata; not killing
you!' Then, when they see that his belly is well extended
from all that liquid, they give him a feather from a cock's tail
and force him to insert it into his throat, '... deep down the
path the poison travelled,' they say to him.

'The man does as he is told. Only, he is so enfeebled by the
heaviness of his stomach and what he'd had before he drank
the *Javel* solution that his attempts do not immediately bring
the required results. Whereupon, the urchins take matters
into their hands.

'"This poison crushes Africa's seed!" they say; one of them
taking the feather from his trembling hand and pushing it
down the man's gullet himself.

'Do you hear what I'm telling you, Mamvulane? Even a
witch-doctor does not put his own hand into the throat of

the man he is helping to bring up poison from his craw.

'But that is what these wretched children did. Put their dirty hands down the throats of their fathers and forced them to regurgitate the liquor they had drunk.'

None too sober himself, Mdlangathi embarked upon a bitter tirade directed at all of today's children, miserable creatures who had no respect for their elders.

Recalling last night's events or the account her husband had given her, Mamvulane now looked down at him; asleep still by her side. Poor Mdlangathi. So vulnerable in the soft early morning light. Poor Mdlangathi. He must have got the fright of his life, she thought, shaking her head in dumb disbelief at the things that were happening these days in their lives.

Her immediate problem, however, was what were they all going to eat once they got out of bed? She had all but scraped the bottom of the barrel last night. Her mind made an inventory of all the food they had in the house: a potato, by no means gigantic; two small onions; a quarter packet of beans but no samp; there was no salt; a cup or a cup-and-a-half of mealie-meal ... And then, there was no paraffin with which to cook whatever she might have, far from adequate as that itself was.

Three weeks now, the consumer boycott had been going on. Three weeks, they had been told not to go to the shops. She was at her wit's end. Mdlangathi and the children expected to eat – boycott or no boycott. Whether she had gone to the shops or not didn't much concern them. All they understood, especially the younger children, was that their tummies were growling and they wanted something to eat. And their unreasonableness, conceded Mamvulane, was understandable. Now, her husband's case was cause for vexation to her. Wasn't Mdlangathi another thing altogether? A grown man. With all that was happening. But still, he wanted and expected there to be no changes in his life. Didn't he still go to work every day? That's what he'd asked her when she told him they were running out of food. What did she do with the money he gave her? As though, in these mad and crazy days, money were the only issue; the sole consideration. And not the very shopping itself – the getting of the food. With the comrades guarding every entry point in Guguletu. And neighbour informing on neighbour. People sprouting eyes at the back of their heads so that they could go and curry favour with the comrades; giving them information about others, especially those with whom they did not see eye to eye about things. Yes, it was so. For the very people who denounced others to the comrades were not above turning a blind eye to the same things ... when the actors were people they favoured. But did her very reasonable, understanding and loving husband, who always gave her his wages, understand that? No. He thought she should just hop on a bus and go to Claremont and there, go to Pick n' Pay! Mdlangathi was something else, concluded Mamvulane, shaking her head slowly like one deep in thought. How did he arrive at thinking, at a time like this, that food shopping was still a simple matter of whether one had money in one's pocket?

The very thought of getting up was too much for her to entertain this morning. Hunger has that effect. Her anger mounted with the growing realization that she faced a hard day with no answers to the questions it raised; that she had to feed her family, and had nothing at all that she could put together and make a meal.

It's all very well for the comrades to stop people from going to the shops, she fumed. They were fighting the businessmen, they said. But as far as she could see, it was only people like herself, poor people in the township, who were starving. The businessmen were eating. So were their families. They were getting fatter and fatter by the day. They had meat and bread and fruit and vegetable and milk for their babies. They put heavily laden plates on their tables ... not just once a day, as most people like herself did in good times, no; but each time they had a meal – several times a day. Oh, no, the businessmen the comrades were fighting were in no danger of dying from starvation. It was not their bowels that had nothing but the howling air in them. And not their children whose ribs one could count.

Mid-afternoon that same day, Mamvulane said, '*I have to do something today*!' As there was no one else in the house, she was talking to herself. Thereafter, without a word even to her very good neighbour and friend, Nolitha, she made her way out of her yard. Looking neither left nor right, away she hurried.

She had her day clothes on, complete with apron and back-flattened slippers. The pale of her rather large heels showing, she flip-flopped down the road. Anyone seeing her thus attired, would have assumed she wasn't going any further than perhaps fifty or so metres from her very own doorstep.

It was a little after three; time to start the evening meal. For those who could do that. Not me, thought Mamvulane bitterly. Not poor me, she said under her breath; walking away as nonchalantly as you please.

NY 74 is a crescent street with three exit points: north, west and south. Mamvulane's family lived directly opposite the western exit, separated from it by two large buildings, the Community Centre in front of her house and plumb in the centre of the circle and the Old Apostolic Church behind it. In reality therefore, from her house she could not see anyone coming or leaving from that exit which lay on NY 65. The other two exits were clearly visible from her house. And usually, those were the ones she favoured because, until she disappeared altogether, she could always turn back and yell for one of the children to bring her anything she might have forgotten.

But this day she slowly made her way towards NY 65; soon losing sight of her house. *'Andizi kubukel' abantwana bam besifa yindlala.'* And thus emboldened by her own thoughts, she went on her way. No, she was not going to watch her children starve to death.

Her plan was simple. And daring. Straight through NY 65 she walked. Into the zones, she went, her gait slow and steady, not once hesitating. Past the zones and into the coloured township of Mannenberg. She'd gained enough anonymity, she deemed. Along Hanover Road she made her way until she found a busstop. With a sigh, she stopped and leaned against the electric pole marking the stop.

Into her breast her hand fished for the little bundle; the handkerchief wherein lay her stash. Money. Busfare and much more.

Carefully, she extricated enough for the fare and put the rest back where it had been; securely tied it into a knot at one corner of the handkerchief. And then back went the purse, safe and secure.

Her wait wasn't long. A bus came. She clambered on – one of only a few still making their way to the shopping suburb at that time of day, and definitely the only woman from Guguletu (or any of the other African townships for that matter) on that bus. The buses coming back from Claremont were full with workers and shoppers returning home.

Mamvulane found a seat easily. Her heart was quite calm. Her chin quite firm. Her head held high. She was amazed at how unbelievably easily she had accomplished her mission thus far. But she knew that the real difficulty lay ahead ... in Claremont? Or would it be harder for her back in Guguletu? *Ndakubona ngoko.* That stubborn thought planted itself in her mind. *I'll cross that bridge when I get to it.*

At Pick 'n Pay the aisles were full. She began to wonder whether the boycott had been lifted and she and her neighbours were maintaining a boycott long past because they had not heard the good news. But a closer look told her the people milling around there were not from the African townships. They were from everywhere else. And what they were doing there, they were doing quite openly – freely and without one little qualm.

Soon, her own timidity left her. She forgot that what she was doing was forbidden. Once more, it had become, to her too, a normal and very ordinary activity. Only the unusual exhilaration she felt, silent laughter of parched gardens drinking in rain after a drought, gave any indication of her deprivation. That, and the serious weighing of choices, which items to select, which to discard and which to ignore completely. Deep down, on another level of knowing, she knew that she had to travel very light.

Her purchases made and paid for, Mamvulane went to the train station. There was a toilet there that she could use. She had put back a lot of the articles that, at first impulse, she'd grabbed and thrown into her trolley. Not unaware of the dangers that lay in her homeward-bound journey, she saw the virtue of ridding herself of most of what she wished for. It would be stupid to make her venture that obvious that she ended up losing all she had risked her neck for. The problem of packaging was of prime importance.

With her two Pick 'n Pay plastic bags Mamvulane entered the toilet at the railway station. Fortunately, there was no one there. In her mind, all the way from her house, on the bus and in the store itself, she had turned and turned the problem of what to do with her purchases that now that the time had come it was as though she had actually rehearsed the whole thing. Several times over.

In less than ten minutes, Mamvulane left the toilet. She now carried only one plastic bag. And it was not from Pick n' Pay. To any eyes happening on her, she was just a rather shabby African woman who might have gone to buy some clothing, not much, from Sales House. For that is what the bag she was carrying said now: SALES HOUSE. And every one knew Sales House was a clothing and drapery store. Indeed, since the bag had long lost its crispness it could be taken that she was a domestic worker carrying home goodies her madam had given her.

Deliberately avoiding the Guguletu bus line, Mamvulane made a bee-line for the Nyanga bus. The line was not that long. Soon, she would be home. Soon. Soon.

When the bus came she was one of the last to board it. But still found a seat, for most workers were already back in their houses, the time being half-past-six.

Ordinarily, she would have been concerned that her husband might get home before her. That was something he didn't particularly care for. Mdlangathi liked to get home and find his wife waiting supper for him so that, should he feel in the mood for it, he could go back out again to get a drink from one of the sheebens nearby. To make matters worse, Mamvulane reminded herself, in her haste and caution, she had not told even one of her children where she was going. Ahh, silently she told herself, I'm sure when he sees where I've been he will not only understand ... he will be mighty pleased.

The Nyanga bus passes Guguletu on its way to Nyanga, for the two townships are neighbours, with Nyanga lying east of Guguletu. Somewhere in the indistinct border between the two, there is an area neither in the one nor the other, a kind of administratively forgotten no-man's land. And there one finds all sorts of people, including some not classified as Africans or as coloured; those who somehow escaped government classification. Some of them work, others don't. No one really knows what does happen in that place, which has come to be called *kwaBraweni*. How it got to be Brown's Place, is a mystery or perhaps a myth awaiting excavation.

Mamvulane let the bus ride past Guguletu with her, making no sign at all that that was where she was headed. Only when the bus came to *kwaBraweni* did she ring the bell, indicating to the driver that her stop approached.

From the bus stop where she got off, it was less than a kilometre or so to her house. But, Mamvulane was well aware that that was where lay the greatest challenge yet. In covering that distance that seemed insignificant and easy.

There was a short cut through a thicket. Avoiding the road, where she risked running into people, she chose the short cut. Here and there she had to use her hands to separate entangled branches of trees so she could pass. Dry twigs scratched her bare legs and she kept her eyes peeled for dog and human shit. Her slippers were old and torn and anything on which she trod would certainly get intimate with her feet.

In the middle of the woods, when she was half-way home, she heard voices, loud enough but still a distance away. Quickly, she stepped away from the path and went deeper into the woods. When she was a good few metres away from the path, she chose a well-leafed shrub and squatted in its shadow. In the case of prying eyes, she would look like someone relieving herself or digging up some root to use for an ailment. Either way, she should be left alone – unless the passers-by happened to be people with more on their minds than she bargained for.

The four-some, two young men escorting their girlfriends somewhere, from the look of things, passed along. They were so engrossed in their discussion that they hardly paid her any heed. If, indeed, they saw her at all.

After they had gone past, Mamvulane resumed her journey, which was without event until she had almost cleared the thicket. She could plainly see the houses to the back of her own, on NY 72, when suddenly her ears picked up a not too far away buzzing.

She stopped to better hear from which side it came. But even as she stood, her ears straining hard to pin-point the source of the disturbance, the sound grew to a cacophony, discordant and threatening.

Right about the time her ears told her to look a little towards her left, in the bushes hiding Fezeka High School from view, her eyes picked up tumultuous movement.

She stood as though rooted to the spot. From sheer terror.

Mesmerized, Mamvulane watched as the unruly throng crowded in on her. Leading the rabble, were a few women and one elderly man. She realized then that a few of those whose heels were chasing their heads were not just ahead of the group – they were actually fleeing from it.

She needed no further notice. Turning from the spectacle approaching her, she ran towards the houses, now so desperately near.

Mamvulane ran. The other women and the old man with them ran also. They all ran. But the army of young people at their heels had speed born of youth on their side.

Just as she came to the T-junction, where NY 74 joins NY 72, she found her way blocked. Some of her pursuers had taken a short cut by jumping over fences from NY 75 to NY 74 and were now ahead of her. In seconds, she was completely surrounded.

Without further ado, someone snatched her plastic bag from her. 'Let us see what you have in that bag, Mama?' he said, ripping it open.

Out spilled her groceries. And as each packet tumbled onto the hard, concrete road, it split or tore open, spilling its guts onto the sand; and there joined other debris that had long made its home there.

Happy and willing feet did the rest. Stamping and kicking at her food so that everything got thoroughly mixed up with the sand and with other food items. The samp and the mealie-meal and the sugar and the dried milk and the coffee and the broken candles and the paraffin ... everything became one thing. All those things, mixed together, became nothing. Nothing she or anyone else could use.

'*Sigqibile ngawe ke ngoku, Mama.* We are finished with you,' announced her tormentors.

Walking home, her knees weak from the encounter, Mamvulane met one of her neighbours, attracted by the noise. "Mvulane, what is happening? Why are all these people staring at you?'

'I can't talk now, Mandaba,' answered the other, not pausing in her unsteady walk. Mandaba, suspecting the cause of her neighbour's reticence and dishevelled appearance, remarked, '*Hayi,* you are naughty, Mamvulane.' To which the latter said not a word; but just continued walking to her home as though the other had not spoken at all.

When she got to her gate, Mamvulane shooed away the straggling group, mostly curious children and one or two adults, that was following her. What the comrades had done to her had disarranged her. But her heart grieved. And that was definitely not on their account. About the comrades, she supposed she should be grateful they had done her no bodily harm. She remembered the man Mdlangathi had told her about the previous evening – the man the comrades had forced to drink *Javel*. That man, after he had brought up little chunks of meat, and of course, the liquor that had caused him all the trouble to start with, had eventually brought up blood. His own. So, when all is said and done, I suppose I'm lucky, Mamvulane told herself after she had calmed down some. At her home. But, her eyes smarting, she could feel her heart bleed. Because of the other thing.

Her husband was home when she got there. 'What happened to you?' he asked, seeing her dishevelled appearance. For, although she had not been beaten, she had been manhandled.

Mamvulane recounted her experience while her husband listened to her in dumb silence. And then she told him, '... and among the comrades who did this to me, there was

Mteteli, our son.' There, it was out in the open. She had mentioned the despicable, unmentionable thing that had gnawed at her heart since the comrades had fallen upon her.

When she said that, mentioned Mteteli as one of her attackers, she burst out crying. Mdlangathi started up and, for a moment, his wife thought he was going to go out of the house in search of their son right there and then.

But no, after two or three hesitant, half-hearted steps, he sat down again and quietly inquired, 'You saw him? With your own eyes, I mean?'

'Oh, why wouldn't I know my own child, even in a crowd.'

'Mmmhhmh.' That is what Mdlangathi said. Only that and nothing more. On being told that his son was part of the crowd that had spilled his wife's groceries on the sand, all that was heard from him was that sigh. That is all.

Mamvulane waited for more reaction from her husband, usually so easy to reach boiling point. But no, not today. Today he kept so calm that his wife became resentful of exactly that calmness that she had so frequently and desperately sought from him. Today, when she least expected it, or welcomed it for that matter, here was her priceless husband displaying remarkable *sangfroid*.

'I'm glad, Father of Fezeka, to see that you appreciate the risk I took, nearly getting myself killed by these unruly children, so that you would have something to eat.' She spoke in a quiet voice. Inside, however, she was seething. What did he think! That she had gone to Claremont only so that she could buy a loaf of bread and stuff it down her own gullet? That would have saved her all the trouble and bad name she, no doubt, had earned herself.

But Mdlangathi would not be drawn to a fight and, after seeing that, Mamvulane soon found her anger dissipate.

When she had rested a little and was sure there would be no follow-up action on the part of the comrades, Mamvulane went to her bedroom and closed the door. When she emerged, in her hand was a tray full of sausage. There were also two loaves of bread and a plastic packet of powdered milk.

'That is all I was able to save,' she told her husband, showing him her spoils. 'To think I spent more than fifty rands at Pick 'n Pay ... and that is all that I was able to save!'

'But how?' He wanted to know.

And she knew he wasn't talking about the money she had spent.

For the first time since she had come into the house, harassed and agitated, Mamvulane allowed a slow smile to appear on her face. Her eyes widening in mock disbelief, she exclaimed, '*Tyhini, Tata kaFezeka*! Don't you think that a woman should have some secrets?' And refused to divulge how she had achieved the miracle.

As she prepared the meal, she wondered what he would say if she were to tell him that she had girdled the sausage around her waist, put the packet of milk in the natural furrow between her breasts and carried the loaves of bread flattened in the hollow of her back, one atop the other so that they formed a pipe. Ah, Mdlangathi, she thought, feeling the smile in her heart, these are not times for one to be squeamish.

But, thinking about the whole *indaba* later as she stirred her pots, now and then peering into this one and then, a moment later, the other one, she was a bit miffed. Mdlangathi had been more upset about the drunkard the comrades had forced to regurgitate his beer than over what they had done to her. Imagine that! A man to have more sympathy for someone like that than for his own wife. She was sure she didn't know what to make of it ... his lack of indignation on her behalf galled her, though.

On the other hand, she had to admit relief that he had not carried on the way he had about the stupid drunk. A fight might have broken out between father and son. Mteteli had become quite cheeky with this new thing of children who had secrets from their parents and went about righting all the wrongs they perceived in society. Yes, she told herself, perhaps it was just as well his father said nothing to the boy ... or didn't show anger on her behalf. Anger that he had participated in her humiliating attack, which had resulted in the loss of her groceries.

Mamvulane dished up and father and children fell on the food as camels coming upon an oasis after crossing a vast desert.

As usual Mteteli had missed dinner; out attending meetings. 'Wife, times have truly changed,' said the husband. 'Do you realize that all over Guguletu and Nyanga and Langa, not just here in our home, people are having dinner with their children only God knows where?'

'You are quite right,' replied his wife. But seeing that he was getting angry, she added, 'but you must remember that our children live in times very different to what ours were when we were their ages.'

'And that means we must eat and go to bed not knowing where this boy is?'

Although he didn't name names, she knew he meant Mteteli for he was the only one of the children not in. The girl, Fezeka, for some reason that wasn't clear to the mother, was not that involved in the doings of the students although she was the older by three years.

'Well, that is what is happening in all homes now. What can one do?'

'Mamvulane, do you hear yourself? Are those words that should be coming from a parent's mouth? 'What can I do'? Talking about the behaviour of her own child?'

'He is your child too, you know? But all these children are the same ... they don't listen to anyone except each other.'

'*Hayi*! You are right, my wife. I don't know why I argue

with you when what you say is the Gospel Truth. Here I am, having dinner when I do not know the whereabouts of one of my own children. Very soon, dishes will be washed. Then we will say our evening prayers and go to bed. And still, we will have no idea where Mteteli is. And you tell me there is nothing to be done about that. Not that I disagree with you, mind you.'

'Well, what could you do, even if you knew where he was right now. What could you possibly do?' Mamvulane stood up, gathered the dishes and took them to the kitchen, where Fezeka and the two youngest children were having their meal.

When Mamvulane returned to the dining-room, Mdlangathi, who was smoking his pipe, said, 'D'you know what's wrong with the world today?' And quickly answered himself, 'All of us parents are very big cowards. The biggest cowards you have ever seen.'

She hummed her agreement with what he was saying. But in her heart, she didn't believe that what he said was wholly true. Powerless, perhaps. That is what she thought parents were; overwhelmed by a sense of powerlessness in the face of the children's collective revolt, where the mildest child had become a stranger: intransigent, loud of voice and deadly bold of action.

'*Mama, kuph' okwam ukutya?* Where is my food, Mama?' asked a grumpy voice in the dark. It was Mteteli, all right. The mother knew at once. Only *he* had not had supper. Only *he* would come in the middle of the night, demanding food when no one had sent him on an errand anywhere that he should have been absent during dinner.

'My son,' replied Mamvulane without bothering to strike a match and light the candle standing on a small, round table next to the bed. 'I am surprised you should ask me for food when *you* know what happened to the groceries I went to get in Claremont.'

'Are you telling me that no one has had food tonight, here at home?' His tone had become quite belligerent.

Before the mother said a word in reply, Mdlangathi roared at his son:

'*Kwedini!* What gives you the right to go about causing mischief that I, your father, have not asked you to perform and then, as though that were not grief enough to your poor mother here, come back here in the middle of the night and wake us up with demands of food? Where were you when we were having dinner?'

'*Awu*, Tata, what is this that you are asking me? Do you not know that a war is going on? That we are fighting the hateful apartheid government?'

'Since when is this woman lying next to me the government? Is this not the woman you and your friends attacked this evening?'

'Mama was not attacked. She was disciplined for ...'

But Mdlangathi sprang out of bed and, in the dark, groped his way towards the door, where he judged his son was standing. Grabbing him by the scruff of his neck, he bellowed, 'She was *whaat*? Are you telling me you have a hand to discipline your mother? What has happened to your senses? Have they been eaten away by intoxicating drugs?'

By now, Mteteli's teeth were chattering from the shaking he was receiving at the hands of his father.

Quickly, Mamvulane lit the candle.

Startled by the light, the two grappling figures sprang apart. Both were breathing rather heavily.

'Are you fighting me?' Quietly, the father asked his son.

'You are beating me.'

'I asked you a direct question. Are you lifting a hand, fighting with me, your father?'

'All I want is my food. I'm not fighting anyone,' said Mteteli sullenly.

'I suggest you get out of my house and go and seek your

food elsewhere. I do not work hard so that I shall feed thugs.'

'Now, I am a thug because I want my food?'

Mdlangathi had had enough of sparring with Mteteli. Abruptly, he told him, 'Go and look for your food from the sand, where you threw it away when you took it from your mother by force.' Fuming, he got back into bed and covered himself with the blankets till not even his hair could be seen.

'Yes, Mteteli,' Mamvulane added, 'Remember all the rice and samp you and your group threw down onto the sand, *that* was to be your supper. You spilled your supper on the sand out there – birds will feast on it on the morrow.'

'*Andithethi loo nto mna, ngoku.*'

'Mteteli, your father goes to work tomorrow morning. Leave us alone and let us have some sleep. You are the one who doesn't have times for doing this or that, you come and go as you please, but don't let that become a nuisance to us now, please.'

'Mama, I don't know what all this fuss is about. All I said I want, and still want, is my food? Where is my food?' Mteteli had now raised his voice so high, people three doors away put on their candles. The whole block heard there were angry words being exchanged at Mdlangathi's house.

Mteteli, angry at the reception he was getting, hungry having gone the whole day without eating anything substantial, approached his parents' bed and stood towering over them, his bloodshot eyes trained on his mother.

'*Hee, kwedini,*' came the muffled sound of his father's voice from under the blankets. 'What exactly do you want my wife to do for you, at this time of night?'

'I want my food.'

'That we tell you it is where you spilled it on the sand, doesn't satisfy you?' Mdlangathi stuck his head out of the blankets again.

'*Andithethi loo nto mna, ngoku.* I'm not talking about that now.'

Under his bed, Mdlangathi kept a long, strong, well-seasoned *knobkierrie*. A flash of bare arm shot out of the blankets. A heave, and he'd strained and reached the stick.

Before Mteteli fully grasped what his father was up to, his father had lept out of bed and, in one swoop, landed the *knobkierrie* on Mteteli's skull.

'CRRAA-AA-AAKK!'

The sound of wood connecting with bone. The brightest light he had ever seen flashed before Mteteli's startled eyes. A strong jet of red. The light dimmed, all at once. A shriek from the mother. In a heap, the young man collapsed onto the vinyl-covered floor.

'*Umosele!*' That is what people said afterwards. One of those cruel accidents. How often does one stroke of a stick, however strong, end up in a fatality? He must have ruptured a major artery.

The boy bled to death before help could get to him, others said.

Yes, the mother tried to get one of the neighbours to take him to hospital, you know ambulances had stopped coming to the townships because they had been stoned by the comrades. But the neighbour refused saying, 'Your son can ask someone who doesn't drink to take him to hospital.' Apparently, he was one of the men the comrades had forced to bring up, forcing them to make themselves sick because they had '*drunk the white man's poison that kills Africa's seed.*'

Of course, later, some people condemned the man who had refused to take Mteteli to the hospital. But others said he taught the comrades a lesson long overdue. And others still pointed at the father and said, 'Why should someone else bother about a dog whose father wouldn't even ask for permission to come to his funeral?'

Yes, many wondered about that. About the fact that Mdlangathi was not denied permission to come to bury his son but had not requested that permission from the prison officials. That was something even Mamvulane found hard to understand. Harder still for her to swallow was his answer when she'd asked him about his reasons for the omission.

'*Andifuni.*' That was all he would say. 'I do not want to.'

However, so did she fear being bruised even more by events that seemed to her to come straight out of the house of the devil himself that she could not find the courage to ask what he meant: whether what he did not want was to come to the funeral or to ask to be allowed to attend the funeral. She did not know which would hurt her more. And did not dare find out.

A Peaceful Exit

Mondli was thirty-nine years old; the furthest thing on his mind, death. Especially his own. Why, only a month before his last birthday, less than six months ago, he had bought himself a car. Granted second-hand but in good repair; the mileage low. The elderly widow from whom he'd bought it had rarely asked to be driven anywhere; the car was practically new.

So was his body. New. Well, *young*.

And his was no ordinary, run-of-the-mill body either. Mondli had been Captain of the rugby team at primary school. He was Captain at high school too. And he was Captain at Fort Hare and later made the Eastern Province Team. He won the most coveted Mr Sports Award when he was only in Form 1; breaking a record that went back as far as records had been kept at Siphumelele High School. MSA belonged to the higher forms – Four and Five. Only once before had there been an upset. And then, a Form Three student had stolen the prize. But that student was as ripe in age as any of the competitors he beat. The year Mondli got the prize, he was only sixteen years old. Almost.

As if to have such a powerful machine were not enough, Mondli was far from wanting in the Looks Department. Gorgeous, he'd heard people say that about himself. And that was nothing the mirror dared contradict. Genetics, a balanced diet, and sheer good luck had endowed him with strong bones well put together, a height that many envied, and skin the term velvety does not quite do justice. 'Ngathi uhlamba ngobisi' – 'It's as though he washes himself in milk', marvelled many in utter amazedness.

A sound upbringing had made sure he was free of vanity; the Achilles heel of many a handsome lad. His father, from early on, drilled him, 'a handsome face is but an accidental arrangement of the bones, my son. One is born looking the way one looks; that is nothing to be proud of, it is no achievement.' The old man told him that so often that he believed it and, as a young man, conducted his life in manner fitting.

And so he had, from an early age, known that test of character lay in one's achievement. As well as one's conduct, of course. He knew that to be admired for looks was not enough to put bread on one's plate. Indeed, to buy one that plate on which one would put one's bread. Therefore, Mondli had applied himself and done well enough in school to please his parents and earn himself a degree and a teacher's diploma.

He made his home with Noluntu, a daughter of the Tolo clan. Noluntu, orphaned early in life, had been raised by several relatives. However, from age eleven till she married Mondli, she had lived with a maternal uncle, *umalume*, and his wife. And, when she thought of parents, it was this childless couple, who had lavished so much kindness on her, she had in mind.

Mondli and Noluntu lived in the township of Zenzele, a comfortable distance from a major city. So they had the best of two worlds: the serenity, safety, and sense of community of small towns and, within an hour's drive, the variety and stimulation a big city offers.

Noluntu was a nurse. They had two children, both girls, Siziwe and Nomahlubi, both in their teens. The girls were doing well in school. Siziwe had only two more years to go, then off to college she would be. Her sister, hot on her heels, would follow her in just a year. Their mother's career was nothing short of stellar. She was called 'Sister' by the township folk. Matron of Zenzele Day Hospital, the only health facility serving her own as well as the neighbouring African townships, she commanded the highest salary in her category. A feat she had achieved in ten short years and despite bitter professional bickering, jealousy, and very small chances for advancement – the usual conditions of small-town black living. But Administration had not done her any favours. She deserved the positions that had come her way. Not only was she well qualified for them, she was a conscientious healthcare provider; diligent and hard working.

On a day that didn't mark itself as being particularly noteworthy, Mondli got up feeling a little queasy, a little tired. He dragged himself to school. As Principal, how could he stay away during examinations? And, in any event, he wasn't feeling that bad and the mid-year vacations were just two weeks away.

Those two weeks were to mark themselves, etch themselves, in his brain with a vengeance. Although he went to school each day, each day he had to take this pill, swallow that mixture, apply this or that ointment. And he developed a need for regular breaks. Just to go to his office – supposedly to rest. But, in actual fact, he whimpered, whined, and cried like a helpless infant the moment he was alone, so crucifying was the pain.

Mondli did not know what had hit him. His wife urged him to see a doctor. 'But darling, we're so busy right now,' he responded. What with exams to supervise, scripts to mark, marks to enter, and results to tabulate, fill in and send off to the Circuit Office? 'It just wouldn't be fair,' he said, 'to take time off and saddle others with my work as well as what they have on their own plates.' And Noluntu, for the sake of peace, decided not to force the issue. She worried though. Mondli, of course, did not know that a violent revolt was afoot ... inside that gorgeous body of his. A silent mutiny. Deadly as sin.

But had his decision been other, it wouldn't have helped the situation at all. Although Mondli didn't know and would later berate himself bitterly, going to the doctor earlier than he did would not have altered the outcome one jot. There are events in one's life that, once begun, have their own schedule, their own timing, their own unfolding. The insurrection inside Mondli's body was such an event. He had absolutely no control over it: the course it would run, or the outcomes it would have. Having started, it would play itself out in a manner all of its own choosing.

Noluntu made the appointment with Dr Madikwa, the family doctor. She wanted Mondli seen by the old man as soon as possible into the schools vacation. And on the evening of the day schools closed she told him, 'We're taking you to Madikwa tomorrow.' And would not listen to any excuse. And Mondli had a few.

He coached the local Junior League Rugby Team. But his wife would hear nothing about his going to practice the next day. Her mind was made up. 'Mr Soloshe,' quietly she scolded, 'you can certainly miss one practice session in your life.'

Reason and a good breakfast made him see sense; see his wife's concern. The sharp stab of pain somewhere in the hollow unknown of his stomach during breakfast added the requisite incentive. Mondli was a little breathless by the time the two got to the car.

'You take the wheel,' he said, wondering if he was not losing his mind. He had never been a good passenger; trusting no other driver except himself.

The doctor's office was like a prison cell but his grasp was firm and reasuring, his smile warm. 'It's only for observation, you understand?' he explained to Mondli, 'there is probably nothing much to worry about, nothing at all.' But he wanted to be sure, he said. 'It never hurts to take a look-see. Besides,' he added, 'you are due for your annual check-up, anyway.'

Noluntu agreed with the doctor's decision and helped Mondli pack his overnight bag. The children were coming early the following week from Elliot, where they were at boarding-school.

But, although Mondli had at first felt that he should wait until they were back before allowing himself to be admitted into hospital, in the end his wife's argument carried the day. 'The sooner, the better,' she said. And he understood. He would get out sooner, the sooner he went in. He couldn't argue with that.

He did want to be out and about before schools reopened. Moreover, what good would he be to anyone, riddled with pain as he was most of the time?

For once the mirror frightened Mondli. He knew that he had lost weight. The doctor had told him that. Not that he had not suspected that something was not quite right, with him. For weeks now, even before the onset of whatever was the matter with him, before he felt any physical discomfort, he had known that his weight was going down. At a rate that should have alarmed him. It had not. Because he had not really paid attention to such an insignificant detail as his pants being loose, his fastening his belt two notches tighter than was usual. And his shoes too, were a little loose, even the new ones.

Together, these and other details were alarming; would have alarmed him. Together. However, Mondli had taken each one in isolation. And alone, each little detail was really nothing that would cause concern to the average, well-adjusted individual.

Mondli had not gathered the growing evidence of his

debility never mind analyse it. He was, indeed, a well-adjusted person. Normal in every way. Caught up in the dazzling vitality of the wave, he totally failed to perceive the vast, agitating ocean.

But once admitted, for the very first time, he noticed that his pallour was ashen. In fact, for quite some time his skin had looked decidedly unhealthy; gone the robust mahogany sheen.

Another detail he had missed. Now, he began to see other tell-tale particulars. His collar bone stuck out, quite quite noticeable. Had it always been that way? he wondered and found he couldn't be sure of how it had looked before. Not absolutely.

What could be the matter with him? Then he shrugged off the feeling of foreboding, telling himself not to be a thumb-sucking sissy.

His first day at the hospital was the most frustrating for Mondli. Time went by so slowly he wanted to scream. He had never been very good at idleness and it irritated him that the doctor who had put him there was nowhere to be found. 'Didn't he say I needed to see to this thing at once?' he grumbled to his wife when she came to see him that afternoon. 'Well, why has he parked me here like a car without an engine, now?'

Noluntu conferred with one of the nurses there and, professional courtesy being what it is, got the information Mondli had for so long tried to wrest from someone, anyone, whoever, regarding when he would be seen by his doctor.

Test after test after test followed. There were blood tests, urine tests, stool tests; and that was just the tip of the iceberg. The physical examination was horrendous in Mondli's mind. That doctor (and the specialists whose aid he enlisted subsequently) who had examined him countless times before, now poked and pulled and kneaded; injected and extracted until, in sheer self-defence, Mondli's body refused to register pain any more. He was just one big blob of flesh with absolutely no feeling at all. Dulled.

Like tactile versions of an echo, he felt the prodding fingers, the blunt instruments, the pricking needles; felt these making their way into and out of various parts of his body. But the feeling was devoid of sensation. Whether it was pain, heat or cold these things were inflicting on him, he could not say. His dermal decoder was at total collapse. His senses were disabled; numbed to the bone.

But even while all this was going on Mondli still was not unduly alarmed. Vexed, yes. And somewhat concerned. But only slightly so. Mildly so.

'I'm afraid I have bad news.'

And so had begun a fierce battle. For the body of the young man. Everything in Mondli screamed NO! How could this be happening to him, he wanted to know. There was no history of cancer in his family, as far as he knew. Both his parents were still alive, showed no signs of departing from this life, in fact. His brothers and sisters, all six of them – three older and three younger – they were all alive and well, thank you very much. Why me? That was the burning question in his mind.

WHY ME?

Plunged into a hell for which nothing in his life up till then had prepared him, Mondli fell back on inner reserves of strength he had not suspected himself of possessing. Now the learning of his earlier years came to the rescue. That ability to stand on one's legs his father had for ever preached, now Mondli found it the only way to go. Those two legs God had equipped him with when he was putting him together. For sure they were skinny and shaky beyond recognition, even he could see that. But they were all he had. And on them he stood. With the help of his vice principal, he ran the administration of the entire school from his hospital bed. And did a lot more besides.

He had had the obligatory second opinion. At his doctor's urging. Same verdict: cancer of the colon. Very unusual in a man his age. That is what both doctors kept saying. And on that point all the doctors, nurses, oncologists and other specialists that would subsequently attend him, concurred. He was just too young to be hit by that particular cancer.

Following the battery of tests and the appalling diagnosis, the doctors put Mondli on a vigorous medical and dietary regime. Exercise. Food. Medicine. And more medicine. And yet more. Those ruled supreme in his hospital life. Why then would he not have hoped ... to be spared? The doctors and specialists and nurses all seemed, to Mondli, to know what they were doing. They exuded confidence. He was in good, capable, and efficient hands he was sure. So sure, in fact, that he began dreaming of going home.

'The cancer has spread.'

For the briefest of time, the words didn't make any sense to Mondli. None whatsoever. But by the time the man in short, white overcoat was saying his next piece, Mondli was fully alert and understood not only the words addressed to him; he understood their implication. Fully.

'It is inoperable and there is nothing more we can do for you here in the hospital.' A heavy silence followed.

'I am very sorry,' the white-clad man's voice was low.

Mondli could not bring his head to nod. Staring straight ahead, his eyes avoided looking directly at those of the man addressing him. At that moment, the Sahara had more moisture than his mouth.

And the man turned his face to the woman beside him. Younger. Also clad in white. All white unlike his white overcoat over normal clothes. She wore a white dress and cap. Only her shoes were another colour. Brown. Even her stockings were white.

'He understands what I'm telling him?'

The man was not even his doctor. What happened? Why had Old Man Madikwa not come to tell him this himself?

The nurse nodded. Three-four, quick and jerky nods; indicating that indeed the patient understood what the doctor was telling him. 'Yes, Doctor,' she said to the already half-turned-away body of the doctor. She didn't tell him the patient was the principal of the local primary school. Instead, her eyes avoiding his, she pummelled his pillows, pulled sheets and blankets up to his neck and, fighting back tears, clipped his chart back onto the pedestal.

He'd paid scant attention to her ministrations; his eye on the receding back in white. He watched it even as it went through the vast double doors at the end of the long hall. The doors swung open, from a push from the man, he realized. There was a brief windowing of scenery from the next ward, much the same as his. Indeed, it was but an unfolding, a rolling on of a screen.

More beds in white. More figures lying prone on those beds. More gaunt and wasted bodies. Then the doors swung to; erasing the scene for Mondli. He was left staring at the blank and sombre face of the double doors. Mondli did not see her leave.

With a start, Mondli saw that the sun was high up in the sky, the morning nearly gone. How long had it been, he wondered. An hour? Two? More? Less? Much as he racked his brain, he could not recall the exact hour of the morning when the doctor had given him the news.

You are going to die.

Not that he had put it like that; but did that matter? What language he'd couched the sad truth in? Did that change anything? Clothing the terrible horror in euphemistic neutrality, an absence of stark reality? There is nothing more we can do for you. Why not come right out and say – The cancer is killing you. And all our modern medicine, advanced science and state-of-the-art technology can do naught to stop it. You are dying even as I speak these words to you? Mercifully, the painkillers he was taking took over and he fell into a deep but restless slumber.

Later that day, Mondli could not keep his tears hidden when he told his wife the news. He did not know that she already knew but had opted to have him told alone, without her presence so that he could tell her himself in his good time. 'He can be very private,' she'd said to the doctor. 'And tends to be protective towards his family.'

'I want to go home.' It was more with relief rather than resignation that he said the words, forced them out of his suddenly numb lips. If he had once believed he knew fear, Mondli discovered he had not known the meaning of the word before. But he was glad to be home, in his own house, among the known and familiar objects and the dear people, who were his heart. There was some comfort in being home.

Although the immediate family was informed of the situation, friends, colleagues and neighbours were told that Mondli was recovering from 'an operation' and would be well enough to return to school in the New Year. Naturally, his parents were stricken. So were hers. They adored their 'son-in-law'. The two girls were concerned at their father's illness. But since they were not fully apprised of all the facts, they were not as worried as they would have been. Mondli's siblings rallied to his wife's side at this very trying time for her; helping in many and different ways, a source of solace to the dying man.

Without their help, the wife didn't know what she would have done. An only child, Noluntu was grateful for the support of Mondli's family (and of course, that of her own). And when she needed an ear, not from the immediate family, it was to her trusted friend, Nomso, that she turned. A teacher at Mondli's school, Nomso had been friends with Noluntu since age six, when the two started school. They had been through a lot together.

The support of his family was crucial to Mondli too. His mind, his heart, his whole being balked at the idea of his dying. Indeed, soon after his return from hospital, with nothing else changed in the status of his health, there followed a period of doubt when his knowing hesitated, hung up there between one footfall and the next; uncertain as to whether, having leapt up from the one, there would be enough spring to propel him forward in such a manner that when he put his foot down it found sure ground on which to anchor itself. Or whether he would slip and slide and tumble down in a never-ending spiral of a fall.

Projects begun at this time remained unfinished, put off, forgotten, too difficult to tackle just yet (as if he could count on the morrow), or were out and out cancelled. These matters were urgent in fact; tasks which everyone must see to in good time – but which assume immense urgency to the seriously ill.

Yet, it was precisely at the mortality they implied that he, unconsciously, bolted. In a vague and undefined way, it was as though were he to not participate in these activities, were he somehow to delay finalizing them, then his life would not be terminated.

Days merged, the one with the other. Time lost meaning. Yesterday. Tomorrow. Today. What did they mean? One large fear obliterated all else. A day. Yet to come; yet to be named. But soon.

Then, suddenly, a glimmer of hope pronounced itself. Quite unexpected it was too. When Mondli and Noluntu had virtually given up all hope, the decline abruptly halted. His condition actually improved. Skin got back its colour; mouth and stomach were again in eager cooperation and Mondli ate full-sized meals that stayed down; flesh grew back and covered the bones it had deserted and he ceased to look like a skeleton. But of all the blessings he could have prayed for, night, once again, became a time of restful sleep for Mondli, who had not had a good night's sleep in what seemed to him like a thousand years.

The seeming improvement fostered a spirit of conviviality in the Soloshe home. The funereal atmosphere that had pervaded the house for months gave way to gaiety approaching carnival dimension. Noluntu was besides herself, to see her husband so miraculously snatched back from the jaws of death. Almost every evening there were visitors, people who had been hungry for a glimpse of the 'Chief', as Mondli's staff called him; fellow congregants from St Cyprian's, the Catholic Church where the family worshipped, where Mondli was christened as a baby, and from where he had married Noluntu. Often, hymns of praise were sung of an evening, when church friends were visiting; many firmly believing that 'where two or three are gathered ...' and grateful that their friend had been spared an untimely death.

The year was drawing to a close for it was the end of October. Noluntu's spirits soared. Where she had feared the approach of Christmas, now she was jubilant, full of anticipation for that same event. She would throw a party such as had never been seen before in Zenzele, she vowed.

When the children came back from boarding-school they would find their father much, much better than they expected. The couple's parents too were exceedingly grateful that their son's life would not be snuffed out when, in their opinion, he had not even reached his prime.

And it was so. Noluntu could not have asked for a better Christmas. The two girls arrived and were soon followed by their examination results. Both had acquitted themselves well indeed, obtaining a Distinction, for Siziwe, and a First Class Pass for her sister. In honour of the successful young women, a sheep was slaughtered. This was just two weeks before Christmas.

For Christmas itself, an ox fell. That big was the joy filling Noluntu's heart that nothing less would have sufficed. And the whole family was with her on that one. It was a time for unstinting celebration – for the birth of the Saviour and the restoration of the health of their beloved; such a wondrous gift.

December 31, Mondli and Noluntu stayed up late. Long before midnight, car hooters blasted, dogs barked a storm, and other sounds of merriment filled the township night. At midnight, the couple went outside to watch the township alight in joyousness, listen to the gasps of the dying year and hear the birth cry of the new. Spellbound, they stood on the porch, silent, each steeped in thought. Arm in arm they stood, in deep contemplation till he broke the silence, 'Who would have thought it possible?'

And there was no need for clarification, both knew exactly what he was referring to. And it was not the scrunch of glass shards tap-dancing on tar or the pungent smell of burning tyres. But the New Year had something else in store. For the Soloshe family. Something very hard to swallow; in wake of such unrestrained jubilation as had been theirs but so short a while before.

The remission, if remission it was, was over. Definitely so. Now the cancer had come back, its strength multilplied a hundred-fold. It more than paid Mondli back for the reprieve it had accorded him. Like a serpent that, having gorged itself to stupor, crawls into a hole and sleeps the winter through only to awaken in spring, discover a huge hunger in his belly and fasten fangs on nearest prey.

This time around, the change was abrupt and drastic. One

day he looked fine. The very next, he could hardly stand without someone supporting him – so enfeebled, overnight, tongues set a-wagging. Where have you ever seen such startling transformation? So sudden? How can the body of an adult, a whole man, lose so much weight overnight?

Worse, even his own parents lost faith in the white man's medicine, wavered in their support of Noluntu's ministrations to him, and finally, picked a quarrel with her.

No one was more surprised than their daughter-in-law when Mondli's father and mother came with the suggestion that they ought to see a witchdoctor about his condition.

'Mondli has cancer. What has that got to do with a witchdoctor?' She knew right there that she was in for a rough time. They would not give up easily, but neither was she going to agree to their proposition.

The argument went on for the best part of two hours and the senior Soloshes left in a huff, quite distressed that Noluntu refused to abide by their wishes.

'What is so wrong, daughter-in-law, with doing what our elders found good for their living?' Her mother-in-law's brows were knitted in disapproval. As hard as she tried, Noluntu could not bring her in-laws to understand that she was not being disrespectful but had no desire to subject herself to a witchdoctor; not when everything in her: her training, her set of beliefs and her upbringing cringed at the very thought of consorting with people she thought of as charlatans.

If Noluntu was wounded psychologically from the battle with Mondli's parents, Mondli's fight with the disease reduced him to a low-level, snivelling-one-moment and hollering-the-next, creature of intense fury and burning hatred.

First, he railed against himself. Why had he not paid heed when the first symptoms appeared? And with the reprieve, what had he done to ensure the illness did not return? Had he been as vigilant in taking his medicine? Doing his exercises? Following the low-fat diet the hospital recommended? This self-flagellation was but short-lived. Soon Mondli's fury turned, full blast, on others – leading all the rest, came his wife of nearly twenty years.

Noluntu's continuing good health offended Mondli. Just looking at her, seeing her well-being, gave him a vague sense of unease, a tinge of jealousy – a queer feeling that she was, somehow, depriving him. Or not suffering as much as she ought to ... at the very thought of losing him. Swiftly, that sentiment changed to a smouldering anger in him, something that he himself did not understand but sensed and felt and accepted as a rightful emotion, quite justified, ... for one in his condition. When not in pain, his thoughts more and more dwelt on the meaning of his wife's character, her love, and her loyalty; above all, her loyalty. That became suspect in his way of seeing things: how could she go on looking like that? As though the most important person in her life was not facing death? Was that her laugh he heard? She could still laugh, dared laugh, while he was virtually in his coffin? Where was this great love she always professed to bear for him? Would such a woman as his wife mourn him after he had gone? Even the recent festivities came under his irate suspicion. Why had Noluntu been so bent on giving him a good time? After all, she was the one in the medical field – had she known that all that hilarity would accelerate his dying?

His anger came out in unreasonable if not downright cruel demands.

'Massage me!' And when the wife rolled him over onto his stomach thinking she would start with the back. He barked: 'No! I want a full frontal!'

'Mondli!'

As well the poor woman was shocked. Full frontal was, or had been, their special term for a special way of getting each other ready before making love. When they felt particularly lovey-dovey. For him to ask for that ... in his weakened condition ... Noluntu fairly lost her tongue.

'I am still your husband.'

'That is not the point, Mondli.' There were tears in her eyes, tears she fought back. 'Please ...'

'*Sihlobo sam*,' thus he addressed her, early the next morning when she brought him his 'mouth-rinse' cup of coffee. There was no answering smile on her face, he noticed. A puffiness around the eyes told him his wife had wept herself to sleep. That is, if she had slept at all, a now contrite Mondli told himself. The poor dear, he thought, she finds the night particularly trying. When he thought of her life after he was gone, left without a husband, a single parent, a woman alone, his eyes never failed to fill.

But Mondli's remorse was short lived. A little later, as he watched his wife getting ready to go to work, again doubt assailed him. After all, he fumed, during the day her work keeps her from thinking of us – of what confronts me. I am facing my grave. Why should I feel sorry for her?

'Aarghah!' he spat out the word and withdrew into a gloomy silence; disgusted at himself for the moment of weakness earlier. Fancy, feeling sorry for Noluntu who stood to inherit so much – his pension; his life insurance; the car he had just bought; the house ...

These days, his brain sought all manner of ways to torture itself. Dissatisfaction, disappointment, and fault-finding; especially with his wife, became prime preoccupations. His children. What would become of them? His wife, with all due respect, was ill-equipped to be a parent – even with him around, her inadequacy was so obvious as to make him flinch just thinking of her alone with the girls. It could not have happened at a worse time, too. His going. With the girls at that troublesome stage of their life – adolescence. How would Noluntu cope without him?

His mother had warned him against marrying a girl orphaned so early in her life. 'Lindiwe is a beautiful young woman, don't get me wrong,' she had told him. 'But orphans, especially those who've been brought up in several families, spoil their children rotten; making up for the lack and hardship they themselves suffered growing up.' Lindiwe was Noluntu's girlhood name. And sure enough, in her eyes their babies were absolute perfection, a zillionth of an inch from angels. The only reason Noluntu didn't accord them full angel status was not because of any flaw she perceived in them. No. She wouldn't blaspheme.

The pain was unbearable. Mondli hollered and hollered all day long. At night, the groans were ceaseless. He wanted to get off the bed, sleep on the floor, he told his wife. 'It is as if my whole body were riddled with hot needles. *Umzimba lo wam wonke ngath'uxholwa ziinaliti.*' Noluntu spread an old bedspread on the floor and, with fresh linen and a light blanket, made him comfortable for the night. As much as that was possible.

Soon, he was so weak, only his voice remained unaltered. He could do nothing at all by himself, the simplest things were too much for him. To sit or stand or walk or eat or turn in bed or lie down if he had been sitting up, all these things were way beyond his strength. But the voice was as of old – booming. Indeed, so unexpected was the robust sound from so fragile a source that the voice was startling, it seemed amplified.

Next, the voice assumed a nature apart, independent, asking for no consent from its owner. Mondli took to making requests that, in the beginning, seemed quite reasonable if numerous. Especially for one whose strength was daily waning.

'I want to see ...' and he would give a name.

'Can you ask So-and-So to please come and see me?'

Thick and fast came the orders. Invitations to Mondli's bedside became the talk of the township. Teachers from his school were summoned. Friends of long standing, some he hadn't seen for donkey's years. An ex-pupil from his early teaching days was requested to make an appearance. Two current students came. A family friend. A neighbour with whom Mondli had had a standing fight for years. And the Priest. The Priest was the first to be called.

His best friend from childhood had once lost money in class when they were in Standard Six. He had been given the money so that, after school, he could go to the Rent Office and pay the month's rent. Mondli received his forgiveness. The man was much surprised by the confession; he had all but forgotten the episode for which he'd been given a sound beating by his father who accused him of carelessness. But even when the incident was fresh, Mondli was the one person he had thought beyond suspicion. Not only was he a friend, he was known to be a good boy who never, but never, got into trouble.

The former student had been expelled from school. Now, Mondli told him the girl who had accused him of being father to the child she was carrying had done that to protect Mondli. If the school officials had found him guilty of getting a student pregnant, that would have been the end of his teaching career.

The neighbour who had fallen foul of the Soloshes had lent them a sum of money. Then, hard times persisting, they couldn't pay it back. Eventually, he threatened Mondli with going to the police. When that happened, Mondli somehow found the money. But, from that day on, would not speak to the man. 'Now, I see that I had wronged you. Please, please, forgive me, neighbour of mine.' And it was done.

The two students were both repeating Standard Four, for the second time. 'What will our rugby team be without you? That is why I did not give you a pass. A terrible, terrible mistake. I will ask the teachers to promote you straight to Standard Six. That way, you'll catch up with your former classmates. It will mean you work doubly hard, but I know you can do it. I am sorry, terribly sorry, my children.'

From his high-school days came another friend, son of a local priest, now a high-ranking official in the Department of Bantu Education. 'We did wrong, my friend. I think you should also confess to our sin. If you were to do the Matric Exams today, you would pass with flying colours, I know. But in view of the excellent work you have done, I'm sure the department will award you the certificate anyway. Or give you an exemption.' The School Inspector was aghast. However, his friend was not quite done. 'And,' he went on, 'ask your father that he seeks forgiveness too, for allowing such a thing to happen when he was invigilating.'

'It is good that Mondli wants to see all these people. He must have something to say to them by way of clearing his way. He doesn't want his way blocked by the quarrels and misunderstandings of this world.' That is what those who heard of Mondli's summonses said. There was a general consensus that he who confesses his wrongdoings before death is a wise man. Mondli, the township people said, was such a man. 'He is not a man whose jaws will be locked in a perpetual open-mouthed scream – a scream from here to eternity because, with his business unfinished, he died fighting for breath … belatedly trying to confess … instead of embracing the journey Homeward.' Mondli, they said, was doing the right thing, asking forgiveness from those he had wronged.

There was a list, slightly longish, of students who failed

examinations when others to whom he had leaked the papers were able to pass. To both groups, Mondli apologized for the unfairness – to the one group, because they later floundered as they had not been adequately equipped to deal with the more rigorous work of the upper standards. And to the other group, for the humilation of seeing their fellow-students, some of whom they knew to be weaker than they, pass while they remained behind.

To his wife, the confession was a double dose of pain. For years, Mondli had been having an affair with the woman who was her maid-of-honour at their wedding; such a close friend she had been, still was, till the relationship chilled dramatically following Mondli's confession. Noluntu, nonetheless, forgave him and although he had asked her, specifically, that she only '... forgive me if you can find it in your heart to forgive Nomso too. Otherwise, your forgiveness is not complete; we have wronged you in concert.' But how could she not forgive a dying man? Would she not then be forsaking her right, with the Almighty, of ever pleading for '... as we forgive them that trespass against us?'

But forgiving Nomso was another thing. Noluntu thought of the confidences they had shared. Had she betrayed her in that too? Told her secrets to Mondli? Not that she kept do-or-die, terrible secrets from him, just little things, the private yearnings of a woman's heart ... but still, she would rather he didn't know about those. And what a rock Nomso had been throughout Mondli's illness. At times, she'd found Mondli trying. And it was to her friend she had turned; especially after the rift with her in-laws. And now? Noluntu just could not get over the double deception. The hurt was just too much to think of forgiveness ... where Nomso was concerned. She would face that later. But she sorely missed the company of her friend and found herself easily provoked to tears.

Some said Mondli left a holy mess behind. 'Strange how mean-spirited he turned out to be in the end.' Puzzled, they asked, 'Why did he have to tell the people to their faces?'

Others agreeing, said there was available after all, old-fashioned confession made to the Parish Priest. Private. And confidential.

Noluntu was sad that, in losing a husband, she also lost the person nearest and dearest to her; someone who would have been such solace to her, now, in her hour of direst need.

However, there were those who saw only courage in the deed. 'If there lives a person who will bear a dying man a grudge,' they said outraged, 'then that's that person's problem. As for Mondli, he will go straight to heaven,' they prophesied. 'He made a clean breast of all his misdeeds and when he left this world, he had made his peace with everyone ... and with his Maker.'

The Widow

At exactly 12 o'clock the service was over. Within minutes, the first cars left the gates of the cemetery. By ten past twelve, the procession snaked its way onto the Main Road: a hotch potch of a coloured, multi-segmented serpent. The harsh summer sun of a Cape noon beat down on it, accentuating its sluggish gait and giving it a chitinous appearance.

In the family car sat Anne Carmichael flanked by her two children: sixteen-year-old Matthew and Susan, aged eleven. Anne chaffed, estimating the return trip would take a full forty minutes, a distance that, any ordinary day, the Audi could lap up in about five minutes. It had taken twenty-five on the way out, as the hundred or so cars, their headlights on, had cruised along behind the forbidding black hearse. The traffic had been far better then.

In the family car, huddled together now as though braced to face some menace, the three held hands. And this physical affirmation of their closeness gave Anne great solace.

We are a close-knit family, she thought to herself; bitterly angry at her husband David for splintering that sacred image in her head. In her heart.

'Everything's going to be all right, my darlings,' she whispered to the children, giving each hand lying in hers a gentle little squeeze.

Until three days ago, she had had no idea of just how much the total picture, carefully cradled in her mind, of her perfect family, did not quite match the reality of its parts.

Behind the dark glasses she wore, Anne's eyelids rolled apart, making room wherein to spread the tears; a trick she learned in her long-ago, lonely childhood. That way, the tears would not spill over the rim of her eyes. They would not furrow her cheeks. Instead, like a blocked rivulet, they would redirect down the walls of her throat: slow salt spreading downwards in little lumps of pain. Like now.

She squeezed her throat muscles, swallowed noiselessly as she tightened each hand holding another – Matthew's left and Susan's right. We'll soon be there, she told herself.

The car glided to a stop in front of the house. They were back.

The driver opened the door on Matthew's side and helped the boy and his mother out before going to the other side for Susan.

Anne's parents, in the car immediately in front of them, were already out and now came to walk them into the house. Her house.

I should be helping them out of cars. Rushing to their side. Not have them come to help me. And this is my house. They shouldn't be ushering me in.

Catching herself, Anne was amazed as her thoughts. Fancy making such casual observations. On such a day. Never had she imagined herself in this role – a widow. But it struck her now that her emotions were not what she would have expected.

As they walked up to the house, groaning trestle tables on the veranda assured Anne the caterers were on time and, for reasons she could not fathom, reminded her of her new situation. They were part of the confirmation she so sorely dreaded.

Widow. From today she would put that cold, dried-up word whenever she completed a form.

MARITAL STATUS: widow

And clerks who did not know her would cluck their tongues in sympathy, their understanding eyes avoiding hers.

She wondered whether she would wear black and immediately dismissed the idea as ludicrous. Which it was. Depraved.

Damn David!

Her face felt like frozen cardboard as, with the tenacity of a seasoned actress who had fallen into disfavour, she guarded her glued-on smile from slipping.

Feeling as unobtrusive as a goldfish in a bowl, she went upstairs to rid herself of her hat and apply a fresh coat of lipstick. Then, down she came, taking in deep pulls of air and bracing herself for the gruelling task of facing the friends who had come to be with her in her hour of direst need.

I need them like I need a hole in the head, she thought, wishing the whole affair were a bad dream, something that, upon waking up, she would laugh off and never have to remember again.

Chin up! she told herself minutes later, graciously shaking hands, passing on thanks, and dishing up smiles.

She had to show everyone she was not disintegrating under the assault of her new and unexpected position.

There were David's colleagues from the University. And his students, his other family.

With a lump in her throat, her eyes alighted on a small cluster. What remained of his family. A sister, with baby and husband in tow. That was all. ALL. Her mind screamed the word in wounded emphasis.

On Anne's behalf, a sizeable contingency from the Black Sash had turned out. She had joined the organisation a few years after her marriage. She was a young mother then; Matthew, not quite a year old. She had found time heavy on her hands, for she had given up her nursing job as a theatre sister soon after she knew she was pregnant.

The idealism of those days! A rueful smile flitted across

Anne's face, dipping the corners of her mouth a quarter inch downwards and filming her eyes. The Black Sash. Champion of the oppressed. Voice of the voiceless millions of Africans. How tirelessly she had worked at the office in Mowbray over the years: explaining the quagmire of apartheid laws to hapless domestic workers; baffled migrant workers; labourers who sought recourse when the law itself was against their ever getting such; families desperately fighting for a chance to live together, to be rejoined when laws had split them asunder and forbade that they live as one. And now, her own family was broken. Beyond repair.

WIDOW. Anne flinched as though a whip had slashed across her back.

WIDOW. Like a one-legged man walking along a small-town road, she would never again be without self-consciousness. Long after the sympathy cards had been put away or donated to the Child Cripple Care society, letters of condolence acknowledged, and insurance money dispensed – gone the way of all money – her friends (and indeed, her acquaintances) would still wear pity in their eyes whenever she was in their midst. That is, those who did not mind her spoiling their table arrangements or who wanted her there because they could pair her off with some awkward man who was alone.

Scanning the faces there, she wondered who, among those present, would turn out what way. She prayed they would leave. At once. And not linger there indefinitely.

Be brave. How long could the tea last? Anne consoled herself. Everyone seemed to be back. People were milling around, some inside and others out on the lawn or on the veranda, for the day was quite warm. Hot even.

Widow. Anne felt a hundred years old; shrunken, shriveled, all spent and hollow inside. As though someone had come and scooped her insides out, tossed them carelessly aside, and then meticulously stitched her up again. What did it matter that she looked whole on the outside when she knew that that was but a shell of who she was supposed to be? An insubstantial shadow of the woman all those present thought they saw? A walking void?

Aloud she said, 'Darlings, make yourself useful.' And put a silver napkin holder in Susan's hands and a crystal pitcher of water in Matthew's.

Pityingly, she looked at them just before she pushed them off and added, 'If you feel up to it.'

She so wanted everything to go naturally.

And it did.

With the help of her mother and father, Susan and Matthew, and, of course, the caterers from the university as well as her own servants, tea was a success.

Anne was pleased with the elaborate affair. We must make it a worthy send-off for a senior member of the Department of African Languages, mustn't we? Uninvited, the far from charitable thought flashed through her mind.

And then the guests finally left. Even the close friends who, meaning well no doubt, stuck like mussels onto a rock, despite Anne's protestations she'd be fine and '... really, you can all go home now. And thanks for coming.'

'Are you sure, Anne?'

As though one could ever be sure of anything under the sun. As though, their being there was not proof enough that she, of all people, would be the last person on earth, from now on, to be sure of her world – shattered as it was. But, people had the right to be absurd, she consoled herself.

She had nothing to say to or think of those who insisted: 'Truly, we've nothing to do. We'd love to stay.' She was merely amazed that they chose to stay with her to do that nothing. God! She had needed her last ounce of restraint. She'd felt like screaming out: Out, Vultures, out! But, instead, she had relied on the tested and tried: staying put exactly where she was; standing by the doorway or nearby. Hovering, really. And not moving an inch back into the house.

Anne smiled when she thought of thick-set Mrs Winslow, David's matronly secretary, whom they called the rhinoceros. Getting rid of her was the hardest thing she'd had to do that day. But even she had had to leave – finally. That naked had been Anne's desire for the departure of her friends. And that starkly expressed.

She'd so wanted to be alone, to make sense of it all. Three days after her husband died, Anne still failed to understand. To see. Let alone to know.

Alone. That was a luxury beyond belief. Well beyond her wretched grasp. Lamentably so.

Mother. Father. Son. Daughter. There were these people. People who could not conceive that they were beyond the point where her own finger tips stopped. Who could not grasp that when she closed her flesh eyes she shut them out. Who failed to know they were part of her world out there, not in. Not her.

The guests had left. The servants retired. And the caterers had carted their wares away. Anne was alone now, with her family. All that was left of her family, minus a big chunk. David. All six feet and more. Gone.

And it was time for the envelope.

Her father handed her the brown envelope he had found on David's desk. Before he'd made the first telephone call after he'd come to her on that terrible day. She was grateful she could always count on her father to know what to do. Under any and all circumstances. He had never failed her before. He had not failed her this time.

'I'll be right over,' he had said, his voice as calm as though this were just a visit like any other.

Only the speed with which he had come revealed that he had sensed her dire distress. She had just not been able to get the horrific words out of her mouth.

But her father had somehow made sense of the scrabbled

garble. Over the distance, he had managed to calm her. And he had taken charge; freeing her from the onerous responsibility. As she had known he would.

Now, she looked at the envelope. No doubt office supplies, she thought, holding it with both hands – between thumbs and index fingers. Pincerlike.

To Anne, Susan, & Matthew

It was David's handwriting all right. The squareness of it. Chiselled. David savaged his letters onto the blank page as one would a stubborn patch of grass with a blunt spade. And yet, the results were not displeasing.

Inside Anne's stomach, a mouse did a double somersault. Her hands trembled and she put the letter down on the gleaming, glass-covered imbuia table around which the five sat. There were six chairs. One was empty. Behind the dark glasses her widened eyes roved around the table, from face to face to face. Slowly. Deliberately.

What did each person behind each face expect to hear? How would she sound, reading? Should she do so aloud? Out aloud? Anne knew she was stupid to even think of the question. What was the alternative? Passing the letter around?

Like pellets during a hail storm, all her fears were upon her – all at once. There was no escape. For more than six months she had known something was wrong. Very wrong. With David.

But this? How had they ever come to this?

Her mind had grappled with the puzzle long and stubbornly as a worm settles comfortably into festering flesh.

Then, three days ago, she had been proved cruelly correct, and David died. Thursday. That was three days ago.

And now it was Sunday, afternoon. Late afternoon. And his letter, a dagger piercing her heart, lay forlorn on the table where her numb hands had dropped it.

She looked at the table, part of their wedding present from

his parents. Both long since dead.

I must be crazy, thought Anne. What is there for me to fear? Hasn't the worst that could happen already happened? She asked herself these questions and others, not expecting any answers. Since David's death, she had asked herself a lot of questions to which she knew there would be no answers – ever. And least of all, from herself. She was all dried up inside. Brain turned to mush. Heart numbed.

Six months of living with terminal illness will do that to you, she told herself. Six long months. And still, I had not realised how serious David's affliction was. Not really. Financial? Career-related? Or what?

Six long months I tortured myself, wondering, scouring my mind with questions: What was eating David up?

And not once did I come even close to the answer.

The legal reforms the Botha Government had embarked upon, to her – as to most enlightened white South Africans – were long overdue. They were more than welcome. Indeed, she was of the opinion they didn't go far enough. Scrapping the Immorality Act was, of course, a good thing. But, with the Group Areas Act still in place, what did it help to allow sex between blacks and whites if, were they to be serious and think of marriage, they would be hobbled and hampered by other laws? Where, for instance, would a mixed-race couple live when the residential areas were still thus legally delineated?

In one swift movement, her left hand reached down and grabbed the envelope as the right hand ripped it open along one of its short ends.

'Careful, dear,' her mother's solicitous voice came to her as from afar.

Anne down-tapped the contents of the envelope and the letter fell out.

Ordinary looking, she noted, not knowing quite what she had expected it to look like.

Upon lifting it, the letter revealed itself a single sheet of cheap paper. White. From a no-name brand packet, observed Anne; remembering that David did tend to go for the cheaper brand of anything he could lay his hands on. I suppose he had a penchant for interior quality, ruefully, she told herself. The bitter taste of aloes lined her throat.

Four pairs of eyes. Focused. On a single white piece of ... evidence? Explanation? Apology? What would it be, to the others, she wondered. What interpretation would each bring to the last words of this man they thought they knew?

Two folds. Three equal parts. Neatly done. The way only David could be maddeningly fastidious about paper. Even cheap paper. As though the thing were living.

Brusquely, Anne unfolded the page.

Someone dragged a chair closer to the table, the screech of its legs on the marble floor muffled, for the bottoms of the legs were cushioned, to protect the high polish of the marble.

Determinedly, she pulled her eyes towards the words hatched on the page. She prized her lips apart. Awoke her tongue. And read aloud for all to hear.

Would her family hear what they so much wanted to hear? The why of it?

Would they hear what she had wanted to hear?

Why?

A scream rent the room: 'No-oo-oooo-h!'

Her imperturbable mother?

The clumsy clatter of a chair overturning.

A startled sob escaped from someone else's throat.

Sue? Or Matthew?

Surely, not her father?

When she came to, Anne was lying on the peacock-coloured sofa in the living-room. Her father, broad back towards her, stood looking out of the French windows. The long, low rays of the summer afternoon poured in and washed down on him, making him look little ... and brittle. As if his bones were made of shells, sickly yellow in colour.

She saw that his shoulders had rounded themselves a little more than usual. And he stood a little less erect than was his wont.

She winced, sensing a great weight crushing him, squeezing life itself from his heart. He had aged tenfold since he had come upon the scene of his frantic daughter and the limp, still warm but lifeless body of his son-in-law. Three days ago.

Her mother, perched on the sofa next to her, tut-tutted and fussed; brushing Anne's hair away from the forehead. With her much-ringed right hand, noted the daughter. She was cooing as to a child, or an invalid.

No sign of either Matthew or Susan. Gone to bed? Watching TV?

Anne wondered what time it was. Now, that was absurd, wasn't it? And, asking herself that question, she knew she had cracked. She was mad. Crazy. What did it matter what time it was? David was gone. Dead. He would never come back. Never. He was gone. Forever. *Oh, David! David!*

'No point in trying to do anything today,' the gentle but reasonable tones of her ever-sensible mother interrupted her thoughts. 'If I were you, I'd try and eat something and then go straight to bed.'

Anne made a face. The very thought of food nauseated her.

'Sweetie, you need to eat something. Otherwise you'll make yourself ill.' Cautioned her mother.

'Shall we ask Jane to bring you something shortly?' asked her father. When she voiced no objections, he escorted her to the bottom of the stairs.

Eyes burned into her back as she climbed up, up, up what seemed to be an interminable flight of stairs. How many were there?

The gaiety with which they had frolicked up and down these same stairs that were thorns to her feet today! She even, then, a little plump, scuttling behind the graceful frame – David – as they counted and recounted the steps until they finally agreed there were thirty-one.

Odd number that, thirty-one. But, there they were, making themselves fall more and more in love with the house. They had decided to buy it by then. The stairs and their number was just one more of several features about it, excuses they had used for making a decision they had already made any way. Prolonging the thrill. Savouring it.

That was ten years ago. Matthew, aged six and his sister, barely a year then, would spend their teen years here. That had been an important component in their decision-making: how the house would grow with the family.

'Teenagers need lots of room,' a beaming David had said. 'They'll have parties and sleep-over friends, you know?' Those were his exact words, recalled Anne.

She remembered how they had talked – she and David – of weddings and grandchildren. And how the house could even take in a son or daughter-in-law (if needs be). A temporary arrangement, of course. Until the young couple could set themselves up.

She gained the top. Without one backward glance, she made straight for the bedroom although she knew her parents stood at the foot of the stairs. Watching. Expecting a wave.

She entered the bedroom.

Our bedroom, said her thoughts.

No. *Your* bedroom.

From now on, your bedroom.

Yours.

Alone!

After a long, long time standing leaning against the door, pure air running in and out of her lungs, not thinking about anything or anyone, blanking her mind, Anne felt her numbness peeling off her. She was regaining herself, she thought.

David had decided to go. He only had himself to blame. He'd had his chance. And spurned it.

By now, late afternoon had become early evening. Anne made her walk to the ottoman. Oyster pink in colour, it stood angled beneath and away from the window which was framed by plush velvet curtains a deep, rich, royal purple. The whole bedroom was done in strawberry shades: from palest pink to deepest indigo. Subtle blending. Hint of this. Splash of that. And any number of gradations in between. The overall impression: colour. Lots of colour. Natural splendour. Opulence. Pleasing to the eye. Restful. Exciting to the senses. Yes, sensuous.

Anne sank onto the ottoman and stared straight ahead although she could see nothing at all.

'Nothing' she told herself in a harsh whisper. Like her life with David. Nothing. That is what her sixteen years of marriage amounted to in the end: a big, fat nothing.

From a distance, she could hear muffled sounds coming from downstairs. Mother talking. Mother always talking. So one or both children had returned to the living-room. Anne wondered which one was the beneficiary of her mother's forever-ready-to-drop pearls of wisdom. Her father had, years ago, escaped into deafness. He was ever careful to see that he never wore his hearing aid around his wife. For a moment, Anne felt a slight edge of guilt that she had left her children to her mother's careless prattle. But tonight she knew she was not up to protecting anyone, not even them, much as she loved them. It was all she could do to go on breathing.

An hour or two later, perhaps three or more – she wasn't sure, couldn't be sure, Anne found herself wide awake. She realised she must have finally fallen asleep. Must have slept secondly too; judging from how she felt … well, wide awake. Or, had a creak as a foot fell on a stair woken her? There was one squeaky step along the stairs.

A soft tap sounded at the door. A pause. Then the highly polished brass knob shaped like a rose bud before it opens fully, turned. Slowly. And as slowly, Anne brought her thickened eyelids together. Almost. She kept her face muscles relaxed, slack and immobile – as those of someone asleep.

Through her slitted eyes she saw her mother glide into the room. Leaving the door open behind her, the newcomer stopped short at seeing her daughter not, as she had assumed, in bed.

'Anne?' She whispered, hesitated and then went on, 'Darling, are you awake?'

Looking at her through her almost clenched eyelids, Anne felt a twinge of sadness at their remarkable separateness. An only child, she had grown up alone in a household of affluence, servants, and two adults, her parents, too preoccupied with their lofty station in life to have room in their hearts for a shy and gawky little girl who was unfortunately neither cute nor pretty. Parents who had never forgiven her for failing to be precocious if she could not be these other things.

At her more charitable moments, Anne felt for her parents who, perhaps through not fault of theirs, were just not equipped for dealing with her ordinariness. And warmth, to say nothing of love or caring ... well, those were definitely beyond their scope: of another world. A world different from the one they inhabited with feverish brio and relish, the smug world of high finance and high fashion.

But maybe she was wrong. Here was her mother saying, 'I want you to know ... we'll do anything to help ... If you want to go away ... for a while perhaps ...'

Pause.

And still, Anne pretended she was asleep. So why did Mum continue?

'Personally, I feel David was a heel. But more than that, and more unforgivable (most men are heels, sweetheart) he was a lily-livered sod. And there is no excuse for cowardice. This mess proves just that. Face up to the fact that you married a cur, my darling.'

'Mother!' so unaccustomed was she to hearing harsh words from her mother's lips that the shout burst full out of her mouth before she realised that it did. Indifference, yes. But not vulgarity. Never vulgarity from her mother. Anne was shocked. Astounded.

'Anne, darling, hear me out. It is better that you face facts now. Postponing that will not help matters at all ... only compound them.'

'Oh, Mum!' And she sat up.

Her mother sat down beside her and took her in her arms; rocking her like a child: to-fro to-fro to-fro, slowly, ever so gently, like a lazy swing blown by tender breezes in spring. Comforting. Reassuring in its lulling rhythm.

'Darling, the least he could have done is to give you some explanation for his cowardly act. Yes, that's what killing oneself amounts to – exceeding cowardice. But no, all he could say is 'sorry ... believe me, I hate leaving you this way'?

The mother's voice had become shrill. Another first for Anne. Her mother's voice was always carefully modulated.

But the other wasn't quite done. 'Who was holding a gun to his head? That is what I want to know.'

Was it those words? Or her mother's wrath and the gentle rocking that unhinged Anne?

Suddenly, her world did crazy cartwheels as a violent upheaval rocked her, deep in her soul.

Down she plunged, down, down, down. Her up-to-then carefully tended calm gone, she looked into the abyss of her soul and knew there was no turning back. For her. She had become unblocked. Her mask had cracked.

Great hoarse sobs racked her.

She clung to her mother as she had never done before, not even when, as a little girl, she'd been frightened or sick or hurt.

Tears welled and filled her eyes. Uncontrollably, they over-
flowed the lids, spilled over and sped down her cheeks to
meet and collect themselves in enormous drops chasing each
other from her pointed chin. The front of the black silk
blouse she'd put on that morning was damp and rumpled.

Wild-eyed and trembling, Anne hurtled backwards
through time.

A Sunday morning. In bed. David tapping her lightly on
the shoulder. Whispering. 'Are you awake, Anne?'

She, turning over. Eyes still groggy from sleep.

Bolt upright the very next second. Pulled up by the fear
deep in David's eyes.

David speaking. The words, hesitant at first then gushing
out, an unruly current from a dam that had burst.

The sordid mockery of a marriage. Betrayal most humiliating.

Mother and daughter. They sat well into the night. The
mother gently rocking her child, the child only black nannies
had ever rocked. The child whose tears the mother had never
wiped away, whose grazed knee she had never kissed better.
And the mother listened to her daughter's far-away voice, the
voice of a scared little girl. A little, small voice, frightened
beyond belief. Frightened and giving fright.

The mother listened. And knew she would have to forget
what she heard.

Unbottled, Anne poured herself out, to her mother. But by
this time, she did not know her at all. What she felt was the
presence of another human being, another person who had
ears to listen, someone who was holding her gently as if she
were a child. Someone she could trust.

She had trusted David too. Trusted him even after he let
her know what a lie their marriage had been; pleading with
her to understand.

'*We have children. The eldest is four years older than Matthew. And there are three others. I must make amends Anne. They need me more than the three of you ever will. They need me desperately.*'

But she'd thought she could make him see reason. If she talked with him. Reminded him of his obligations not only to herself. Not only to their children. But to society at large. He had his teaching career to take into account. There were other people to consider, she reminded him. Her family. Moreover, whatever would happen if every other husband took off after a mistress, deserting his lawful wife and his rightful place in society?

She had been prepared to forgive and forget, let bygones be bygones.

But David had looked pityingly at her, as though she were the one at fault, the one demented, the one who should be forgiven.

'You don't understand, do you?' And, helplessly, she had looked at him, a prayer in her eyes.

'Now that the government has finally taken a leap into the twentieth century, I want to do the right thing by her ... and *my* children.'

'Please, remind me,' a voice she didn't recognise had croaked out of her mouth, a frightened frog's voice. Then, choked with emotion, she continued, her voice steadily rising, 'Who is the father of *my* children? What is his duty to *those* children?' She was screaming now; the words tumbling uncontrollably out of her mouth. Her whole body was trembling from the tumult of feeling welling up inside.

At that point, David lost his temper and yelled, 'Damn, Anne, put yourself in my position. The big liberal, hot shot academic, going about condemning the Nationalist Party and its dehumanising policies. How would I be any better if now, given the opportunity to be with her, after twenty years of clandestine and furtive meetings, I shun my duty?'

She had known then that she had to switch the contents of his bottle of insulin, that he, a diabetic, would be using to inject himself. He was leaving her no alternative. She had to do her duty. She was a theatre sister; knew what to do.

Looking at him; hating him as she had never known she could hate anyone, the simplicity of it all almost made her laugh.

'David was leaving. He was leaving *me*. Leaving the children. I had to stop him ... just had to stop him. He would bring disgrace to all of us.'

Derisive laughter erupted from Anne's throat. Full of venom. Spiteful like a witch's cackle.

'Goodbye, David, Goodbye!' she said, quietly at first, as though talking to someone quite near ... someone she didn't want to disturb. Someone at sleep, perhaps? Or just resting?

Soon, however, the goodbyes came with increasing loudness. And faster and faster they came, with each repetition until the words ran into each other and formed a garbled, incomprehensible salad.

'No need to go into details in the letter, David, spare the children. If you can find that much compassion left for them.' Stroke of genius that, the woman had to admit to herself.

And darling David. Darling, trusting David. Trusting. As she had trusted. Ever predictable. Sensitive. Caring. He had agreed. Never realising how angry she was. How hurt. How humiliated.

How did he think she would ever show her face again? Left, not for another woman, no; but for a black peasant?

The laughter and the tears and the words pouring out frightened the mother into endless motion. She rocked the woman–child to-fro to-fro to-fro with increasing tempo, to match and drown out the furore raging from her ward. She was aghast at what she heard and knew she had to forget. Forget and never, ever remember she had heard. And pray her child woman who said those horrible things would never remember saying them at all. Never remember knowing them or doing them at all.

But, in her mind, the child saw the things the mother wanted her to forget. David. Reaching for his syringe. The syringe he'd filled with what he thought was insulin.

Injecting himself.

Lying down to read.

Feeling the numbness as the Pavulon took effect.

'How could he think of doing such a thing to us?' Anne hissed, arms flailing as fists boxed unknown demons in the air; demons only she could see.

'I had to stop him!' She screeched. 'I had to stop him, didn't I? He didn't know what he was doing. He was crazy! Crazy, I tell you! Leaving me for a black woman!'

The deranged woman jibbered on and on, unhinged with jealousy or, who could say? memory too painful to contain.

The mother, subdued and numbed with shock, rocked her frightening child, hushing her, hush-hushing her ... well into the fretful night.

Now, the child saw David's look of utter consternation as his muscles grew numb, useless as meat on a butcher's block. Why, she could see that he couldn't move even his eyelids.

'*Damn David!*' jumped straight out of her mouth, her face contorted as her mother continued to rock her on. Cooing softly. Soothing the demons raging inside her woman child's mind.

It was almost daybreak when Anne finally fell into an exhausted, fitful sleep.

The mother tiptoed to the door. Gently, she opened it, and beckoned to her husband at the foot of the stairs.

He came up, taking the stairs three at a time, his step light and lithe.

Outside the slightly-closed door, the two conferred conspiratorially.

A few minutes later, he called the family doctor.

Anne woke up firmly ensconced in a private room in a nursing home. Flowers filled every available space. Soon, she had been told, she would be ready to go home. Soon. She would be with her children.

She was almost fully recovered. Severe state of shock. Trauma. Her husband taking his life like that. Poor woman. A widow. So young. Pretty too. Only thirty-eight years old. Young. Too young, to be a WIDOW.

The Hand That Kills

'You are a despicable creature. Not only have you taken an innocent life, done so in cold blood; but you committed an act of bestial betrayal at the same time, killing the very hand that fed you.'

The judge droned on about how he was to be taken from where he stood and locked up in a cell from where he would be led out 'to be hung by the neck until dead'.

Dumfounded, Lunga listened as if the words had nothing to do with him, not really. Someone was going to wake him up from this terrible nightmare; tell him everything was all right; no one was dead. He, Lunga, was not in jail facing the hangman's noose. But, above all, tell him Mr Walker was alive. That is what he wanted to hear more than anything else in the world. That was more important to him than even his stupid life. He would not mind dying really, if only Mr Walker, dear, gentle, kind Mr Walker, were alive and well.

His mother was out there somewhere. He had seen her earlier, seen the pinched look on her face. Like him, he knew she could not believe what the police said had happened. What they said he had done. What he did not deny had happened. Only, how could it have happened? How could he have done what they said he had done?

The guards led him away. It was with relief that he walked between the two men in uniform, walked away from that place. Any place would be better, a haven. This place where he had listened to horrible details of acts attributed to his hands was unbearable. Hell!

Mother must have fainted. Or died. He had expected to bear her scream any minute during the proceedings; but more so at the sentencing. Surely, that must have been hard for her.

Silence.

Where his mother's heart-felt sorrow should have rent the courtroom air, a deafening silence. Lunga could not understand the silence of the mother he knew was grieving. For the shame. The sin. The incredible, horrible murder of which her son stood accused and now convicted and sentenced. The death of her master. Lunga knew the pain of the faithful servant was undoubtedly excruciating.

And the Prosecutor had accused him of showing no remorse. As if that would bring the man back. As if all the tears that flooded his heart could change a thing. Stupid bastards didn't even know the meaning of sorry. They knew absolutely nothing and understood even less.

Three days. Three whole days of torture. Days he was in hell. Lunga could not see why the damn thing had been dragged on that long. He had denied nothing. 'A very co-operative witness', the Prosecutor had called him. So then, why did they need all these experts?

One testified regarding the exact moment of expiration. Another, the angle of the bullet's entry, its trajectory, and other causes contributing to the fatality. Yet another gave details about loss of blood and implication thereof, especially on someone of Mr Walker's age. There had been no call for that. Not in such a 'clear-cut case' – according to the Prosecutor himself.

The nearer the end of his short and pitiful life, the more his mind flung him back into the past, into the intolerably uncomplicated days of his past. His childhood. All the happiness he was ever to know was back there.

Slouched on the small, hard, wooden bench in one corner of his tiny cell, he was once more a little boy and Mama was urging him, 'Come on down from that swing! We're going home, now.'

Home. Strange thing that. Home was not home although it was the only one he knew. The only one he had. His mother called it that and so he too called it that. They had no other. Except, it wasn't theirs. Not really. Never had been. And never would be.

His mother had worked for Mr and Mrs Walker since she was fifteen years old. That was some time before she became his mother. An orphan, she had had to leave school and fend for herself at that early an age. The Walkers had no children of their own and when his mother got married, they gave her 'the most beautiful wedding a girl could dream of'.

She continued to work for them after she was married. His father had worked in a restaurant in nearby Claremont. Although the marriage did not last long, it had lasted long enough to produce him.

He had never met his father. Didn't even know his name.

'You better believe me, my child, you are far better off not knowing him.' That was all he ever got from his mother, the few times he'd asked tentative questions about the man who had fathered him. And the Walkers, who practically raised him, were of little help in this one respect.

Mrs Walker, when she was still alive, would wrinkle her long nose, close her eyes as though preventing herself from seeing some unpleasant ugliness and spit out: 'Mean scoundrel, if ever there was one. The way he treated our Sally, here.'

They called his mother Sally, did the Walkers. Her given name was Selina. She often boasted that she was named '... after the beauty queen of the Fifties, Selina Korai. Because I was such a beauty as a baby!'

And she had faded clips of her namesake. *The Beautiful Selina Korai.* That is how the caption went. And beneath that was a picture of a smiling woman. He supposed she was pretty; but he would not have put her in any beauty pageant himself. His mother now, hers was real beauty. Stunning. She had truly astounding looks. And he was not saying that just because she was his mother. Oh, no.

Mr Walker loved taking him on drives and the boy enjoyed that better than the swings and merry-go-round at the park where Mama sometimes took him during her afternoon-off time. Sitting in the car and watching buildings, and later trees and sky, whizz by was great fun. And always, Mr Walker would buy him ice cream or cream doughnut, things he absolutely loved. Sometimes he would stop at the OK Bazaars or at Ackermann's and get him a brand new toy: a water pistol or a car. He had no sense of unbelonging then. He was a child and knew no other home except 16 Tivoli Avenue in Newlands.

You are the son I never had.

And it was the naked truth that no man had taken more interest in him while he was growing up than Mr Walker had. No man. And he had never asked Mr Walker about his father. Not once.

'Lunga! Where is that lazy boy? Come here, you. See if you can run faster than Bingo! Get the ball!'

Of course, only later and after many trials to outrun Bingo with all his might, did Lunga understand that dogs are just naturally faster runners than boys. But he'd given the uneven race his best shot. Whether or not this had anything to do with the fact that he later became such a good sprinter, no one could say. He liked to think it did.

He roamed the Walker house freely from when he was a baby right up to his teens. There had never been any restrictions, barring the normal, if irritating, boundaries adults set for children.

Naturally, he grew up more fluent in English than his own mother tongue, Xhosa. And when the adults, his mother and one or both of her employers or just the Walkers alone, when they didn't want him to hear what they were talking about, they used Afrikaans. Until he went to school, he didn't have a word of Afrikaans. But he had a flair for languages and it was not long before he was able to grasp some of what was said. It took the adults longer to realise he understood what they were trying to hide from him.

'If he has all those other children, then I never want to see him. He is not my father!' Lunga had given himself away, on that occasion; stung by the hard-to-grasp fact that the shadow that lived only in his imagination, the man he had so long dreamed of meeting one day, was in all probability not eating his heart out, anxious for such a meeting. If he was just one of his *''n honderd kinders'* as Mrs Walker had said, then why should a man like that be pining for him?

'How many times have I told you that you are a bit too smart for your own good?' one of them said. His mother? Mrs Walker? He couldn't say.

The two women had been talking about the child-support money his mother had not received for six months in a row. Apparently, with that many children, the man had decided it was more profitable for him to stop working rather than pay child support. That evening, his mother told him, 'Lunga, we should count our blessings, my child. What does it matter if I don't get any help from your father? We have ...'

'I told you, he is not my father. I don't have a father. And I don't want to hear anything about him, ever!'

And she had never again, not once, mentioned that hateful man.

In his own mind, the boy, more and more, began to think of Mr Walker as the man who was his father. Why not? Hadn't he said so himself, said that he thought of him as the son he never had?

Occasionally, his mother made vague allusions: They would never want for anything. Mr and Mrs Walker had promised her they would see that he got a good education: became a teacher. They would buy her a house in the township one day; when the time was right. Even if she were to die, her kind employers would never turn him away. This was their home, the Walkers were as good as parents to her. She was very lucky indeed. Both of them were.

Before he could walk, Mr Walker had started buying him comics and books and read these to him. And when he started school, he made a big fuss about his school reports: showering him with praise for good, even half-way good, performance. And chastising him for remarks from teachers which said he was lazy or did not apply himself to his work. Mrs Walker was a great one for the occasional cookie or sandwich between meals; even sweets: chocolates or some other delightful, delicious tidbit. But for horsing around, a boy could have no better companion than Mr Walker.

Into this Eden, Time – cruel, thieving Time – had brought unforgiving consequences. Lunga's growing into young manhood would have been a challenge at the best of times. But the times were far from best. To add to that, he was not only growing into young manhood but into *black* young manhood. And then, there were other circumstances.

First, Mrs Walker died in a car accident. This shrank Mr Walker's world which had not been a vast one to start off with. To all intents and purposes, entertainment ceased at the Walker home for, as Mr Walker himself would say: 'Who would want to visit a crotchety old man who lives alone?'

More and more he came to depend on Sally.

At this time, he would have liked to do more things with the boy, as he continued to call Lunga. But the latter had struck up a friendship with Roy, a boy who went to school with him, and so he spent almost all his spare time in

Guguletu. And all the things he had previously enjoyed with Mr Walker, he now found extremely embarrassing. None of his Guguletu friends went fishing or mountain climbing or bird watching or clearing the mountainside of invading foreign flora. As a consequence of their out-of-sync social situations, just as Mr Walker's need for his company grew, Lunga's desire to distance himself from the man was growing too.

'Sally, do you think the boy is avoiding me?' came often from Mr Walker's disconcerted lips. And the mother could only exclaim in denial: 'But, of course not, Master. He is not.'

Deep down in her heart, however, the mother feared her Master's suspicion was well founded. If not all the truth, still sufficiently so to cause her much grief. She just did not understand what had come over the child, so stubborn he had suddenly become.

The day before Lunga was to go to Langa to apply for his pass, Mr Walker told his mother: 'Tell him I'll take him there.' He would have told Lunga this himself had the young man been home.

True to his word, Mr Walker was ready to drive Lunga to Langa the next morning; but the young man had already left. His mother did not relay details of the fight they had had.

'I don't want *him* driving me to Langa, Ma!'

'Why are you being cheeky? Mr Walker is only trying to help you, you know?'

'Help me get a pass?'

'You know what I mean. He has things to do, he is a very busy man. But he will drive you there in his car so that you will not spend hours and hours on the buses and trains or waiting at the station. Also, with him, you will not be made to stand in the long queue. They don't let white people stand in lines.'

'Well, I am not a white person.' And with that he had

abruptly left. Not even bothering to say goodbye.

She didn't have the heart to tell Mr Walker how rude her son had become. So she mumbled something about friends he was meeting who were also going to apply for their passes. And this was true. In part.

What the mother did not know was that her son had been recruited to be a member of a newly-formed group of militant young students from the townships of *Langa*, *Guguletu* and *Nyanga*, the LAGUNYA PANTHERS. This was the nucleus, the yeast that was about to ferment revolt among young Africans throughout the country. The year was 1975. And it was December.

The group's mission was simple. Dangerously so: raising the consciousness of African students to their plight as students and to the plight of the masses of which they were an integral part. The codicil was crucial. Hitherto, the educated African had tended to see the proletariat as something apart from himself, a group with which he had little in common and which, out of enlightened pity, he might labour to uplift.

A few weeks after Lunga had been given his pass, he was on his way home after a LAGUNYA PANTHERS meeting when he was stopped by the police who demanded to see his pass. He gave them the document which they duly examined. Then one asked him where he was going that late at night.

'Home,' replied Lunga. It did not occur to him that he should give an explanation. But to the policemen, his answer was a clear example of cheeky behaviour. His nose would have been pointed in the opposite direction, in their reckoning, were he on his way home.

'You think we're here to play games with you?' snarled one of the policemen. And WHAM!

Instinctively, Lunga struck back; he had not had time to think, to fully grasp the meaning of what was happening. However, that was soon remedied.

In no time at all, the police made tenderised steak out of his

face and then handcuffed him and threw him into the back
of a van.

It took three full days of frequent telephone calls to all the
police stations and hospitals in the peninsula before Mr
Walker found him. His mother had already asked her
employer to phone the mortuary too; which he had done.

Both his mother and Mr Walker were much relieved he was
alive. Mr Walker made quite a fuss at the police station;
demanding to know why the police had not notified him of
the boy's arrest. The Sergeant on duty, who said he knew
nothing of the case as he had not been on duty the evening
of the arrest, apologised for what he called 'this unfortunate
misunderstanding'. But he was also quick to point out that in
view of the peculiarity of the case, the error, on the part of
the officers concerned, was understandable.

'Sir, you have to see it from the point of view of the poor
policemen. When the young man said he was going home,
how could they know he was not one of these *skollies* who
go about breaking into people's houses? We have a lot of
complaints about the *Bantus* who are always going up and
down around here. This is a white residential area,' he
reminded him emphatically.

Mr Walker thought it best to leave well alone. He knew
what the Sergeant was doing: reminding him that, in fact, by
keeping Lunga on his premises, *technically*, he was breaking
the law.

Lunga resented having to carry a pass. He resented even
more having to 'produce it on demand'. This episode only
aggravated that sentiment and fuelled the fury long smouldering in his heart.

'You wouldn't understand,' he hurled at Mr Walker shortly after the pass incident when the latter, in an ill-advised
attempt to ease the youngster's pain, likened carrying a pass
to carrying an ID book.

'It's not the same thing and you know it!'

Later, at a meeting of LAGUNYA PANTHERS, Lunga spoke with feeling about the hypocrisy of the liberals.

'You know what this white man used to tell me? *"You are the son I never had"* and I swallowed that shit. I believed the bull, ma'an!'

'*Ja*, those people are good at sweet talk. But when it comes to action, the best they can do is promise. They should be called *Promerals* instead of Liberals!'

'*Promerals*! I say, that's cute.' One of the group of young men guffawed and the whole band broke out laughing. Then Lunga interjected:

'Let me tell you something else. We have been *promeraled* a house. I don't know where or when. But, according to Mama, we are getting a mansion from our *promeral*, one *shushu* day.'

What had made him remember the house? Mama had talked about that ever since he could remember. What had brought it to his mind just now? The others were wiping away tears of laughter. Lunga too started to laugh at his own joke. At the absurdity of believing in the myth. Till then, he realised, till that very moment, it had never occurred to him the house was nothing but talk. Cheap talk. And he was sure his mother believed she would get the house. And that made him so angry he wanted to squash something; take it in his bare hands, wring its scrawny neck till it stopped breathing – if it were a living thing. Or, in the case of a non-living thing, crush it till no one could tell what shape it had been before it got acquainted with his angry hands.

His eyes darted to his hands, open and idle now, lying lifeless on his lap. These hands that had committed the terrible act.

Lunga looked at them. At his hands. And still found it hard to believe what they had done.

And they had no anger when they did that. No anger at all. Only fear. Fear at its rawest. Blind terror churning his guts and filling the back of his throat with smelly sour milk that had gone bad. The foul smell and the sour-bitter taste of acid rolled into one. God! How everything had gone all wrong that day. If only he could roll back the time; go back to any time before that fateful day. This time, he would surely take a different path.

The riots that had started in Soweto in June that year hit Cape Town a month later and, of course, Lunga took part in the rupture. All high school students did. And the LAGUN-YA PANTHERS had specific orders. As a lieutenant in that organisation, he had a definite role.

At home, however, neither his mother nor Mr Walker understood any of what was taking place. His mother, plain-ly bewildered, demanded: 'Have you all gone mad?' Pain and anger filled her eyes as she looked at her son as if she had never seen him before, as if he were some strange creature from another world or, as if his hair had changed to writhing snakes right before her eyes.

And an equally befuddled Mr Walker told him, 'I am thor-oughly disgusted. Here is your poor mother, working herself to death to put you through school, and this is how you thank her!'

A few weeks into the boycotts, the feeling, very strong, was that he should get a job since he had obviously left school. But that was out of the question. 'The People's Soldiers' were not allowed to work. They were called to higher duty: organ-ising the masses. His massive vocabulary and oratorical prowess made him a natural for giving speeches. And the leader of the group had chosen him for this task.

However, with the indefinite continuation of the school boycotts and the sporadic riots, problems cropped up and threw the LAGUNYA PANTHERS into disarray. Sworn secrecy sprang leaks like a sieve; discipline gave way to arro-gant self-seeking behaviours and the fire-spitting serpent, jealousy, wiggled his way into the very heart of the organisation.

Then one day, during a post-operational meeting, the leader singled out Lunga, praising him for a job well done and went on to say he was loyal and brave. At this, one of the members of the group called out, 'Let him prove it!'

The leader's steely stare failed to silence the disgruntlement. Instead, other voices joined in and a murmur of discontent rose: 'Yes, let him prove it! Anyone can talk, let him prove himself; some of us have!'

Lunga's status with the group, living as he did in a white suburb, had always aroused a low level of resentment. On that day, the hostility erupted into the open. And the leader decided to put a stop to the rivalry, which he felt uncalled for.

During the discussion that ensued, it came out that most of the other members felt Lunga had done little to deserve the job he had been given; a job both glamorous and high in visibility.

'He needs to be baptised in the fire of action,' voiced a veteran of many skirmishes.

'Let us see the colour of his courage!' another added.

And Lunga had listened as they discussed his 'Mission', the task he would perform to 'prove himself'. Several ideas came up and were tossed aside: Too easy. Irrelevant. Unnecessarily risky. Dumb.

'What about your white-man father!' piped up a faceless voice.

'If you can do that, you can do anything that will ever be required of you.'

And, just like that, it was agreed. Going to his white-man father's house would make him a worthy lieutenant in the eyes of the members of the group. 'Then, we will know that you are a soldier.'

'Maa'an, that is when I should have stopped the whole silly thing. Right then and there!'

The words tumbled out of Lunga's mouth without his being aware he had said them aloud. The sound of his voice shattering the stillness of his cell sent a cold snake slithering down his spine. With a sigh, he closed his eyes.

Eyes closed, a video of that terrible scene flashed right before him; vivid as any he had ever watched with Mr Walker. His inquisitor, however, wore his mother's face. Strange thing that.

Yes, I went there with a gun.

Yes, I knew it was loaded.

Yes, I knew that Mr Walker lived alone.

Yes, I knew that, it being Thursday, Mother wouldn't be there.

Suddenly, there was a clamour as a thousand disembodied voices, all at once, blasted his ears away.

It was your intention to kill him! Was it not? Your intention to kill him! Intention. Intention. Intention to kill. Kill him!

NO! NO! NO! A thousand times. NO!

He had not expected Mr Walker home. Why did they not believe him?

Why had he carried a gun then?

Lunga swallowed hard. But nothing went down his parched throat.

How could he begin to make them understand the pressure he had felt himself under? What did they know about fighting to gain the respect of your comrades? He'd had a plan. Certainly, he would go through the motions. But for him, this had been more to show off to his comrades, show them he was as capable of bold action as the next person.

His plan. So simple.

He would have returned with the loot; tell eager ears how he had made the white man grovel, plead for his life. And how he had terrorised him into submission. But, in reality, he would just have 'borrowed' the items. That's all. Borrowed a few of Mr Walker's possessions. Things he hardly ever used. It would be years before he discovered they were missing. He might even die without ever knowing they were gone. That had been his plan. So simple.

Only, the day took its own sweet turn; changed his plan and left him holding a body.

He had been more shocked than Mr Walker when their eyes clapped on each other. *The man could not be in the house. He was away. In Pinelands. Playing golf. Today was Thursday!*

But, even then, things might have turned out far better than they did. Why had Mr Walker grabbed the gun? How could he have believed that he, Lunga, could actually shoot him? How could he believe such a thing? After telling him so many times: *You are the son I never had?*

And then, the stupid gun went off.

Lunga, covered with blood, screamed; fearing he had been shot; fearing he was about to die.

Soon, however, he realised his terrible mistake.

Fear swiftly gave way to a sinking feeling as millions of little worms gnawed frenziedly at the walls of his stomach.

Cradling Mr Walker, Lunga had slumped onto the cold, unyielding floor, unseeing eyes staring into nothingness, mouth wide and dry as the desert, body bereft of feeling.

And that is how, hours later, his mother had found the two.

The Sacrificial Lamb

Before Siziwe was fully awake, the receiver – cold, hard and decidedly unfriendly – jabbed at the not-fully-awake flesh in the hollow between her shoulder, the pillow, and her ear. She did not remember how it had got there. There was a vague memory, of the phone ringing; but even as she had struggled to hold it, sleep had left her in frustrating confusion with a tantalizing overlap between reality and dream. But, of course, the phone must have rung, otherwise why had she picked up the receiver? And now, to the remote peep-peep announcing an overseas call she mumbled, 'Hello?' – relief washing through her. It was not the police, calling about her daughter, Fezi. She glanced at the bedside clock-radio thinking, *where, on earth, is that child*? Just then, a voice came through the line.

'Hello? Is that you, *Sisi*?'

'Yes, it's me. Who is this?' She no longer recognized the voices, her nieces sounded so grown to her whether on the phone or in their infrequent letters. No doubt, Siziwe was sure, distance and nostalgia accelerated and augmented the changes she perceived: with them ... with her.

'Is everything all right?' she asked; a new anxiousness replacing the earlier worry. What if her mother were ill? What would she do then? Go home? Or sweat it out here till ...? What would be the point of going then? But even as she argued with herself in her mind, she knew: of course, she would go.

'*Sisi*, it's me, Nozipho. Everything is fine; after a manner of speaking, that is. What else can we say?'

'What has happened? Is Ma okay?'

'Mama is okay. She says can you call her back?' And before she could say yea or nay, there was a clang and the line went dead.

She leapt out of bed and went to make herself a cup of coffee. Might as well make myself comfortable, she thought. Calling Cala was never a simple operation. The call had to go via the telephone exchange ... and the Cala Telephone Exchange was slack and inept, and often the lines were down.

The coffee burned her throat the way she liked it. Her mind went back to that long-ago day, the day she had not known would be her last for her to see her father. One would have thought there was a way of feeling, of sensing, of somehow presaging such an event; a kind of body seismograph, reading her the foreshadowing symptoms. But no, despite her great love for him, she had looked at her father, talked to him and then walked away from him with a casual goodbye. Next thing she knew, the sturdy tree that had given her shade from scorching sun and shelter from the storms of life had fallen.

On the second attempt, much to her amazement, she got through.

'Hello, *Sisi*? It's still me, Nozipho. There's something I forgot to tell you.'

'Yes, Zips? What is it?' she tried not to think of the money she was paying, listening to idle chatter. Sheer waste.

'I have written you a letter and given it to *Bhuti* Wallace. He is coming there and we gave him your address and telephone number. Please, Sisi, do respond positively to my request. Do not disappoint me, you know I have no one else I can depend on.'

'What is it?'

'No, I can't say it now. Wait till you get the letter.'

'That bad, is it?'

'No, it's not!' A burst of thrilling laughter fractured her speech. '*Sisi*, I must get off this phone.' Siziwe knew what was coming. She could hear her mother grumbling in the background. 'Ma is giving me her wicked look. You know her. Bye, Sis'.'

'Bye!' Had she heard? wondered Siziwe for her 'bye' collided with her mother's 'Hello, Siziwe!' as belaboured breathing replaced Nozipho's breezy prattle on the line.

'Hello, Ma! Are you all right?'

'Siziwe, my child, the Lord keeps on minding us. But the devil is also busy, derailing us every which way we turn.'

'What is the matter?' And she had the presence of mind to stop short of adding the 'now' burning the tip of her tongue. But the irritation seared her brain. *Can they never call just to see how I am doing? Is each telephone call always only going to be about some catastrophe?*

'MaTolo is in hospital.' There was a slight pause, no doubt her mother waiting to hear her reaction to this piece of news. But Siziwe waited too ... Whatever she said would end up upsetting her mother; she did not seem ever to come up with anything kind to say about her eldest brother; a complete wash-out of a man.

'Our kind neighbour, Majola, took him to Gunguluza Hospital in his car.'

'What is the matter with him?' This time she was forced to say something since her mother had gone silent on her.

'We really don't know what happened to him. Saturday, early evening, some people came and told us that he was lying face down, at the corner of NY 1 and NY 3. When we got there, we couldn't even recognize him. Half his face had caved in, probably hit with a brick – what they call the Wonder Loaf here. He was completely covered in blood that had already caked. As yet, no witnesses have come forward to say who did what to him.'

'But what about him? What does he say happened?'

'He can't even say one word, my child. All he does is groan. He does not even recognize those who have been to see him. I, myself, have not been to see him; could not bring myself to go ... no, I just couldn't go and see him looking like that ... like a corpse.'

'I am sorry, Ma. I'm really sorry.' And, to her surprise, she realized that she meant what she said. Of course, she was only sorry for the worry MaTolo's troubles always caused her mother. Her sisters and brothers were slowly killing the poor woman; aging her and wearing her down fast with all the troubles they visited on her: drunken brawls, job loss caused by bad work habits, unemployment due to lack of qualifications, and a host of other causes besides. The same problems that plagued everybody else in the black townships ... why did she allow these things to disarrange her? Why would her family be any different from all the others?

Once more, her father's words of farewell led her to a decision. Often had she wondered whether they were a blessing or a curse. '*Mna, kuphela eyam intlungu yeyenyama.* My pain is only that of the flesh.' Thus had he thanked her ... or, perhaps ordered is more like it ... for those words had forever after directed her actions ... especially towards her mother.

Even so far away, in this strange land, among people whose ways were stranger still, she still heard those words. *While other men in this ward cry, not because of physical pain but because they do not know what their children will eat that very day or a man's family is being thrown out of the house* because *they owe rent money, I am at peace because you, my daughter, see to the needs of the family.*

'So, we thought we should ask for some help from you, my child.' Her mother's voice broke into Siziwe's reflections.

'I know we are forever bothering you with all these stupid problems these children are always getting themselves into. But, what else can we do? Who else can we turn to?'

There was a moment's awkward silence. The unspoken words ... 'Now that your father is no longer here' ... heavy between them.

Had her father, in thanking her for giving the family financial support, in fact appointed her his surrogate?

'You must help us, my child.'

'Of course, Ma.' She was embarrassed. 'What did you think I should do?' Of course, that too was just formality. She knew exactly why they had called her ... why they always and invariably called her: Money.

'Whatever little money you can send us, will help. We have to go to the hospital to see him. What would people think ... and how would he feel? We can't abandon him there all on his own ... and at a time like this.'

The next morning, a Monday, she got up half an hour earlier than she usually did. She liked to start her work day punctually and purposefully; more so Mondays. She was dressed and getting ready to leave when a groggy voice asked her, 'Want a cup of coffee, Mother, dearest?' Siziwe did not trust herself to say a word in reply. But the look she gave Fezi was more eloquent than anything she could have come up with.

By nine, she had made the transfer from Chemical Bank to her mother's account with Volkskas Bank in Elliot, the nearest town to Cala that boasted such facilities as banks. Over a cup of coffee, she thought about Fezi. *Hope she makes it to class.* When the girl had eventually found her way home the previous night, Siziwe had no idea. Mama's call had come well after two; nearer three than two in fact. And after the call she had gone to see whether Fezi was in her room. Not getting a reply to her knock, she'd gently pushed the door open. And the serene bed so incensed her, blind tears rolled down her cheeks before she even knew she was crying. How many times had she told the girl, 'All I ask, is that when you are busy having fun, I should not be lying awake in bed, wondering if the next telephone call will be the police, telling me you've been shot or strangled; raped, robbed or pushed in front of a moving train.'

But her daughter behaved as though the mother were a big fuss-pot. As if these horrendous things were not happening, every day, in the city where they made their home. As if they were something Siziwe just conjured up to frighten herself and use to chain her daughter to the house. But then, that is the privilege of the young, the singular lack of fear of death; completely believing in their own immortality.

After work, she stopped for Happy Hour at The Ritz, a cozy little restaurant patronized by the foreigners because of its international cuisine. She was meeting Nomsa, a fellow South African who had lived in New York for almost thirty years. As usual, before long their talk was about home, the country, its people and, more particularly, their families.

'Hey, Siziwe, do you want to hear the latest about my crazy family?' When she nodded her head, knowing full well that whether she wanted to hear Nomsa's news or not, hear it she would, Nomsa told her, 'My sister is unbelievable! Do you remember her?' There was a pause but not for long. Nomsa answered herself, 'I've told you so much about her, you must. This is a woman, over forty, who dropped out of university. She is so bright, she had a first class matric pass, passed the first two years in college with flying colours, but then, despite our advice, despite our protestations, decided she wanted to get married.

'Well, of course, that didn't last. Two children. No profession. Too proud of "My University Education" to do any job unless it is not beneath madam's status.

'Doesn't she call me, collect? Do you know how many times I have told her not to do that? Unless, of course, it is absolutely necessary: a death or grave illness, something of that nature.

'But no, each time she goes on a binge, she remembers she has this rich sister in America and calls me, but I have to pay for those calls. She is not that drunk she forgets that an overseas telephone call costs a lot of money.'

'I also had a call from home yesterday ... or, early this morning, I should say.' Siziwe interrupted, still smarting from the hole the morning's withdrawal had made in her savings.

'Ah, but your family, listen to me, your family is reasonable. Mine? Mine, is something else, believe me!'

Siziwe started to tell her about her mother's call. Then, somehow, Fezi's staying out the whole night, ' ... for she must have come in well after four – came in and took centre stage.

'I miss having my family help me with the children. You know, at home, this wouldn't be just my problem alone. Her uncles, my brothers, would help. So would Mama. She would talk to her, show her how to behave herself.'

'Yes, that's true,' replied Nomsa. 'Our extended family is truly a blessing. One is never alone, whatever travails one is facing.'

Siziwe nodded her head, thinking of her mother and the strength she drew from her, just knowing she was there. Whatever would she do if anything happened to her mother? She told Nomsa, 'You know something? Often, when I'm troubled, I will pick up the phone and call Mama. But, when I hear her voice, realize how far she is, I ask myself: Why should I bother her with my little troubles? She would only worry. And the Lord knows, she needs that like she needs a second head on her shoulders. And, do you know what? Just hearing her voice; just knowing she is there, I already feel better.'

'Remember what you said, some time ago?' Nomsa was

looking at her expectantly.

'No. What?' Which of the numerous things she had said to Nomsa over the years was the other referring to? Well, Nomsa would just have to remind her. Siziwe waited, eyebrows raised in question.

'You said, 'Those of us who are supposed to have "made it", are the ones whom, for whatever reason, the ancestors have chosen as sacrificial lambs for the family!'

'Oh that? Sure,' said Siziwe, 'but this is slaughter! And when will I save for old age? Things are changing and I would be a big fool if I expected my children to look after me when I am retired.'

'Very true, my friend. But, as you yourself have said, we are helped to be successful, so that the family may endure. How else would so many of us have survived apartheid ... were it not for those who, despite overwhelming odds, "made it" to where they could support us?'

Bhelekazi's Father

It was not his height that made him odd. Not the great big army coat he wore come rain or shine. Not because he often carried his daughter in his arms, something none of us children big enough to walk ever got from our fathers, or mothers for that matter. Not because he was Bhelekazi's father and no one else's. No. No. After all, there was *Tat' uShortie*, the location dwarf, to beat him hands down, on the first and last counts. However, Bhelekazi's father was the subject of our youthful curiosity from the very beginning, when out of nowhere he and his wife and little girl had appeared and moved into the unfinished house next to ours. And that is what set him apart from all the other fathers in New Site Location, Retreat: the house. Remarkable, that tiny house was.

That was indeed a feat in New Site Location, where uniformity was the order of the day. Oh yes, we could tell our shacks apart. But, how much variety can you get from cardboard, nail, newspaper, sack, and zinc? Roof: peaked or flat. Zinc: new or rust-coloured. One or two windows. Two or three bricks or a concrete slab pretending to be a step just outside the door. One woman who had no children even had a thick rectangular 'mat'. She put the folded and stitched sack there so that people could wipe the dirt off their feet before coming into her house, which was always, but always, neat and tidy – plank floor scrupulously scrubbed spotless and gleaming, the colour of dry bones. But truth is, on the whole, the outstanding feature of life in the location was the comforting sameness of the place; a sameness that was pervasive. Except, as I have already said, the house of our immediate neighbours, Bhelekazi's family.

Their house was different. I cannot tell you now and I know I didn't know then which of the houses in New Site Location was the biggest (who was measuring?). But that Bhelekazi's house was the tiniest in the location, we children all knew. And everything in the house was shrunk to size; as if the people in it feared any article a bit on the large side would upset the harmony of their dwelling or in some way overwhelm them.

Often, because the place held immense fascination for me, my eye would sneak a glance from the doorway (I never once went inside that house) – whether plate or spoon, broom or knife, blanket or water drum, everything up to the little bed hugging itself over there by the corner – everything was small. Even the little three-legged black iron pot was smaller than any I had seen. Not that I'd seen that many, mind you. No one used them in the locations any more. Our homes boasted Primus Stoves and silvery shiny aluminium flat-bottomed pots with black plastic handles that defied heat.

We called the house *icala lendlu*, half of a house. Which I thought quite apt and fitting, because that is precisely what it looked like: unfinished. As if Bhelekazi's parents had started to build a house, finished what was to be the smaller bedroom (assuming there were to be two) and then, for one or another reason, stopped awhile. And just never got around to continuing the work they had interrupted. Never added that other room: bedroom, dining room, or whatever. The inside wall, all cardboard and plain, unpapered; raw as a wound still healing, waited. And waited. And waited ... On rainy days we wondered how Bhelekazi's mother kept the little room dry. But then, birds' nests, flimsy to the eye, were as dry as dry can be inside right after a heavy rainstorm.

I may have found the description *icala lendlu* appropriate but that is a view my mother did not share, as I was to discover one day.

A group of us was playing *blek blek mampatile* and I was the 'eyes closed'. When I had counted up to one hundred, as the rules stipulated, I opened my eyes and started searching for the others. After a while, I had found everybody but Nozakhe, a clever little thing that, I swear, could turn itself to thin air so that you'd never find her till you were forced to give up. That is exactly what I was about to do when, with the help of unconscious give-away glances from the rest of the group, I spied her lurking behind *icala lendlu*.

'I see you! I see you, Nozakhe. Behind *icala lendlu!*' I cried out at the top of my voice. She came out of hiding; and I had a perfect game.

Blek blek mampatile is an evening game. So it was not long after this before we all headed home. Mother greeted me with sorrowful eyes. What have I done now? I wondered, anxiously going over my daily chores in my mind. I'd fetched the water from the public tap. I'd brought in the baby's napkins, folded them and put them away. I'd swept through the front room. What special job had she asked me to do that I'd forgotten all about? Nothing came to mind. But I knew I was in for a high jump; the looks she was giving me told me I was in trouble with the law. In our house, the law had lodged itself in the person of my mother long before we were born. Father was only the execution wing of the law. Mother presided over cases, heard arguments, judged, and passed sentence.

Father had not even washed his weary feet, something he did every evening when he came home from work, before Mother pounced on him:

'D'you want to hear what your daughter has done today?'

As we never 'did' anything unless it was something we

shouldn't have done, the question confirmed the fears I'd had ever since I'd walked into the house earlier in the evening

'*Mmmhhhm*?' I could hear Father's tiredness in his voice. But Mother would make him listen. And act, if she thought that he should do so.

'This child has a mouth that will surely land her in jail one day; let me tell you that.'

'What has she done now, again? *Uyawenze ni*?'

'Doesn't she call our neighbours' house names? At the top of her voice, too?'

Then she went on, telling him how she was busy cooking the evening meal when, she heard my voice, loud and clear, '... people as far away as the avenues could hear her, I'm sure.'

The avenues were miles away from the tin-shacks we called home. They were real, tarred streets with pavements, imposing buildings, electric lights and cars zooming up and down them. That was where we did our grocery shopping. From Indian and Chinese shops.

Both Mama and Tata were looking at me. I wished I could disappear although, to tell you the honest fact, I still did not see what wrong I had done. Yes, I knew she was talking about *icala lendlu*. But what was so bad about that?

'Why did you say that?' Father asked after Mother had told him what I had called Bhelekazi's house. Listening to her say it, the innocent-sounding name took on an unsavoury tinge. She made it sound dirty, a swear word.

I could see Father's heart was not in what Mother expected him to do. The trouble is, Mother sensed his reluctance too.

'It is said that a tree must be bent while it's still young, you know? If you let her grow wild, don't blame me one day when she lands in the high court in front of a judge!'

Crime and sin were synonymous in our community and had clear-cut gradations. Appearing before a judge labelled one as a beyond-repair sinner, incorrigible; just waiting for the day your sad soul left your body, going straight to hell.

'Why did you call Mbhele's house *icala lendlu*? Are you going to answer me or must I take the answer out of your hide with a switch?' Mother's words had roused father to action, all right.

And all I could think of is, 'It won't happen again. I am sorry, *Tata*.'

I got a long talking to. Father showed me why it was wrong to say 'hurtful things to others'.

'You see,' he said, sitting me right opposite to him so that he could look me straight in the face to see that I was minding what he said. '... what you say makes the other person feel bad about their situation. Then they blame God for putting them in it.'

Father told me that when that happened, God would be displeased, not with the people who blamed him but '... with you ... for making them blame Him.'

I didn't quite understand how what I'd said could trigger such a serious chain of events; but I was not going to argue with him, I was in deep enough waters already.

In a voice from a mumps-infected throat, I promised never to call the house that name again.

'It's better not to say unkind things at all, at any time, to any one.' Mother said; and both Father and I knew the case was closed, the judge had summed.

I heard great reluctance in her voice. Father may have been too tired to give me the hiding she felt I deserved, she was reserving the right to bring the case up as soon as I gave her the slightest excuse to do so. Why else would she go from this one specific case to talking about 'any time' and 'any one'?

The next morning, and every time after that, when I looked at Bhelekazi's house and remembered my promise to Father, I failed to understand how my parents could not see the house as I saw it. My eyes saw what they saw. No one would convince me otherwise; the house was but half a house. Henceforth, I just took care never to say *icala lendlu* anywhere near where Mother might hear me or in a loud voice. And often, I would simply say, '*icala*,' and let whoever I was talking to complete the phrase in their own mind. Which none of my friends had the slightest problem doing.

Bhelekazi's father was odd in other ways too. He looked old although neither his hair nor his beard had any white in it. His voice was low and slow. His eyes seemed always to be looking at things not so near, things only he could see ... vaguely. He looked older than Tatomkhul' uMxube, the oldest man in the location. And Tatomkhulu had stopped work long before any of us children were even born. But, I swear, his gait was far brisker than the shimbling shambling of Bhelekazi's father.

Her mother was a tall woman, heavy-boned. She had a full, round face, gentle eyes and the barest hint of a smile always hovered somewhere in that face ... but just never got itself to be born. She had an air of weariness about her that made you feel a little sorry for her, without knowing why you did. She looked far too young to be the wife of this much-aged man. But perhaps that was only because her husband looked so old. I don't know. That Bhelekazi was their only child, did little to lessen the oddity of this family. You will agree that that was strange indeed, among people where ten or twelve children was not that uncommon.

Also, Bhelekazi was, or appeared to us children, too young for a couple that old. Why had they married so late, we asked ourselves often, for we believed they were older than most of our own parents (or at least as old) and there was Bhelekazi, the youngest of the children in our little group.

Both parents were gentle in movement and in speech. So we envied Bhelekazi for having parents as gentle as those;

what if they were old? They were not the least bit crotchety. They never scolded her. They never raised their voices at all, in fact. Her mother was the only mother we knew who never, but never, cried out aloud, screaming her child's name, calling her home to some chore. Yes, Bhelekazi was one lucky little girl, we agreed among ourselves, for we never heard a voice raised from our neighbour's little half house.

'That is a singularly silent house,' even the grown-ups often remarked. Very little sound ever came from it. The people in it seldom spoke, in fact, and when they did it was in voices subdued; just a little above a whisper.

Bhelekazi too, was far from a rowdy child. Understandable, I suppose. With parents such as she had, how could she have been otherwise? She seldom spoke. Her voice too, was soft, a mere hush in fact. Always, one had to strain hard to hear what she said. Mostly, though, she gave a barely perceptible nod in assent or shook her head from side to side, just once each way, to indicate disagreement. She was much praised by our parents. Now, there is a child who knows her place and never talks out of turn, they said. Truth is, she just never said anything at all. Or did so so seldom as to make no difference.

If her parents never raised their voices scolding her, Bhelekazi gave them no reason to. Timid, she never wandered far from her mother's side. Unless you call a metre or two from the doorway an adventure into the great wilderness.

While Bhelekazi's parents kept to themselves and seldom opened their mouths, the rest of the location had a lot to say about them. Only, most of what they said came out in whispers, especially when we children were around. Of course, this only made us even more curious about this family than we already were.'

The woman of the little house never bothered her neighbours at all. She wasn't one to borrow matches, salt, or paraffin; common practice among people who never had enough, to whom the phrase self-sufficient was a complete stranger, unknown. In her little house with its little objects, she seemed to manage just fine. Imagine my surprise, therefore, the day I saw her come over to our house. Imagine my utter astonishment when I heard her ask mother: 'Mother of Lulama, are you going to use your oven on Friday?' Adding, 'I ask only because, if you are, I would like to share the space with you ... if I may?'

Mother told her, 'Certainly, you can come and put in your bread. I am baking tomorrow.' She was visibly flustered. Her neighbour had never said more than 'How are you?' to her before.

Bhelekazi's mother apologised, saying the only reason she asked was that she had more than two loaves to make. At this, Mother's brows shot up. 'Are you having a feast?'

'No,' replied the other. 'On Saturday we will have people. They are coming to give us *umchamo*. We are leaving on Sunday, going back to the country.'

Saturday. The morning wore the radiance of a bride. The blue sky blushed early in the day, for the summer sun rose long before the milkman's whistle. Here and there the air lost its coolness as it gathered sweet and heavy scent from a nearby bush.'

Mother offered to help her neighbour in making the provision the family would take on their journey. Before the guests had started arriving, she made a coal fire in 'her oven', the big metal drum lying on its side and almost completely submerged in sand. Over the bright red coals, she put an iron grid and thereon went seven loaves of bread in rectangular pans, a whole chicken and a leg of mutton, which Mother had bought for our neighbours. Thereafter, the mouth of the oven was sealed with a heavy sack, first soaked in water. The whole contraption, tin and sack, was then covered with sand;

completely buried.

By mid-morning, a sizeable group, mostly men, was seated around the missing part of Bhelekazi's house. Bunks had been hastily borrowed from the neighbours and were now arranged in a neat horseshoe. The normal hush of the little house was replaced by a constant din as of bees in a large, overcrowded hive. Smoke from the men's pipes rose into the air and formed a haze above their heads. There were shiny metal beakers circulating around them. *Umqombothi.*

'What *is* happening at your neighbours?' amazed passers-by asked mother that day. And she told them what the occasion was, adding, 'They only have *umqombothi* though.' And I sensed censure in her words. Only the poorest of the poor would call people to their home and not give them liquor as well as *umqombothi*, for although the white man's liquor was still forbidden to the African then, its use in the locations was not at all uncommon.

As the day wore on some left but more came. Those who worked on Saturday did so only until noon. So the party really got going only with the lengthening of the shadows.

We all knew what the gathering at Bhelekazi's meant. Yes, we were a little sad for we knew we would never see our little friend again. Very few of those who returned to the country did we ever set eye on again. But, in the nature of childhood calamities, our little grief was overshadowed by the abundance of the day. In the locations, it was true that when the adults partied, the children had a feast. Not only were the adults more generous on such days – Here, take this penny and go and buy yourself a *vetkoek!* Here's a tickey, get some sweets! But they forgot about daily chores and we children got extra play-time that way.

This day, even my strict parents did not remember to call me home until long after the usual time. Dusk had already given way to real, no-nonsense dark.

After church the next day, the little house next door

already looked deserted although, in fact, there were two people too many there. The men, Bhelekazi's uncles, her mother's brothers, had come to see the family to the train station of Cape Town. Everything in the house was already packed.

One battered little suitcase stood just inside the door. The adults sat huddled together, no doubt going over last minute details about the whole sad affair of departure. Bhelekazi too, although of course, she was not part of the discussion, sat near her parents; silent, as usual. Play was out of the question for Bhelekazi that day. She was so cleanly scrubbed the pale edges of her feet were clearly showing. She wore the less faded of her two cotton print dresses. She was definitely ready for the road.

Finally the time came for Bhelekazi's two uncles to accompany the family to the train station in Cape Town. Out of the house and down towards the outskirts of the location the little party made its way, onto the sawdust footpath that led to the tarred road a good three hundred metres from the location. They neared a bend that would take them clean out of our sight; we waved our sad goodbyes to Bhelekazi, who seemed frightened or shy and didn't wave back. She did give us one or two furtive little backward glances though. And then, the throat of the road swallowed them up and we could see them no more.

Monday. By the time we came back from school, the news was all over the location. Of course, now, a lot of people in New Site Location said they had always known that under that silence the man hid the heart of a *skelm*, a beyond-redemption rogue.

'Fancy doing such a dirty thing to such a decent, good woman who never talked back to her husband? A woman who did not drink? A kind, quiet woman, who ...' Mother stopped short when she saw me come in. But MaMkwena,

Neo's mother, to whom she was talking, had not finished.

'What I would like to know, Mother of Lulama, is what is going to happen to the little girl?'

Mother shrugged her shoulders, '*Hayi*, God will see she comes to no harm. But, as for that man, he is either mad or possessed by the devil.' And, with that, announced it was time she saw to her pots, meaning she had to start cooking. MaMkwena left; but I knew that what they were talking about was Bhelekazi and her father.

Indeed, we knew, from the word go, that the 'diabolical man' was Bhelekazi's father. What we could not lay our collective finger on was what he had done. Grown-ups are terrible that way. They will talk in riddles until one's head is confused with all sorts of gory details.

By the time Father returned from work, dinner was ready. Mother wanted an early night, she said. She'd worked hard all day and was '... tired to the bone.' She didn't fool me one little bit though.

That night, the whispering from my parents' bed was vigorous. Father, who could never whisper with the deep voice he had, threw out one question after another. He must have exasperated Mother for, at one point, I heard her clearly say, 'Well then, choose what you want to believe. But what I'm telling you is the Gospel truth.' Father said or asked something after that, and Mother, in almost normal voice, driving her point home, said, '*Asingomkakhe wokuqala lo*. This one is not his first wife.'

'*Sshhsh!*' urged Father, too late. Did I have a biggie to tell my friends? I couldn't bear the long wait till next morning. I eventually fell asleep, the whispering still going on in their bed. But it had become too faint for me to eavesdrop profitably.

Comparing notes the next day at school, I gathered that the whole reason Bhelekazi's family had left, was because the clan, the extended family in Cape Town, had decided they were not doing that great in the city and it would be better if they returned to the country, *where one does not live by wages but by what is planted and reaped*. His brothers-in-law, particularly, found Bhelekazi's father wanting, regarding the manner of his providing for his family. '*Akanantsebenzo*, He is not making it,' they said, according to what one of the group had been able to glean from the adults' conversation at her home. And so, it was felt the whole family would be better off back in the village.

That was good enough, except it left unanswered the question of why the mothers were worried about Bhelekazi, and the riddle of who was not the first wife. And how did all these details belong, how did they fit together?

Then, three weeks later, I hit the jackpot. It was Mother's turn to host the women's *mgalelo*. Once a month, several of the mothers got together and put their money together and gave it to one of the members of their *mgalelo* club. This way, each had a turn of buying something significant, something *that one can really see*, that's how they put it, *into ebonakalayo*, something tangible.

Now, the members of the *mgalelo* club didn't just come into someone's house, throw the money on the table and leave. Oh, no. These meetings were a social occasion, a little tea party, for the twelve women concerned. And so, Mother needed me to help make and serve the tea and biscuits. I had never, before that day, shown such enthusiasm for the task.

You see, I knew that there was no way even Mother could keep a dozen women from talking for two hours and more. Not that dozen, at any rate. Especially now that there was a juicy piece of news in which all of them were so interested. And the fiasco Bhelekazi's trip turned out to be was definitely such an event.

And sure enough, before long, tongues were wagging. And my ears were burning, there was so much for them to take in, and all at once. And this is what I heard:

The money made during *umchamo* was good; enough for a grown-up's ticket from Cape Town to Cofimvaba, where the family hailed from. Not that anyone thought that was what it would be used for. Money from *umchamo* was really a little extra friends and family gave to those returning to the hardship of the moneyless rural areas. It was meant to help, certainly. But, not even in the buying of provision, although that is what it was called, *umphako*. There were numerous problems whose mouths were wide open in the country areas, and one was never at a loss as to what to do with money there. But everyone was expected to have, at least, the money for the tickets and what he would be eating during the three-day journey home.

When the party had reached Cape Town Station, Bhelekazi's father left his wife with her brothers while he took his daughter and went to buy the two tickets. Bhelekazi was too young to need a ticket. She had not even started school.

The train was already in the platform. Cape Town, a terminus, was the beginning of its route. The wife's brothers helped her secure a place for the family; putting suitcase and provision basket on seats to stake her claim. They were travelling 3rd class where there are no reservations and one has to jostle for a place.

The three adults stood huddled close together as the brothers gave last-minute messages for their own families back in Cofimvaba.

One of the brothers looked up just as the longer hand of the big black clock on the platform jerked, leaping to eleven. 'Where is *Sibali*?' alarmed, he asked, for he saw that only five minutes remained before the train pulled out.

'I'll go and find him,' responded the other brother.

Panic struck the little group, the woman and her two brothers. 'Perhaps the lines are long.' He ran down the platform, disappearing in the same direction his brother-in-law had gone a while ago.

In a flash, he was back, rivulets of sweat streaming down his face. '*Andimboni. Akakho phay' ematikitini!*'

The woman took two-three steps forward, nearing the train. People were rushing all over the place; a veritable pandemonium. Her husband might come at the last minute, she thought. She must be ready to jump in.

'You are right, sister. Maybe you should wait for them inside. They will be here any second now,' advised the brother who was still puffing from his sprint. But the other brother would not hear of such a thing.

'No! No! You can't get in,' he screamed. 'You have no ticket. And what if he comes back too late? The train will leave with you. What will you do then?'

Now, the minute hand was right on the twelve, making a lean, long, straight line with its partner, the shorter hand. But Bhelekazi's father had not come back from buying the tickets. His wife was frantic. Her brothers were annoyed at his tardiness. All three had eyes on that part of the platform where they thought he'd reappear.

Just then, the conductor's whistle blew announcing – ALL ABOARD!

Next, the train gave a phlegmy *ssshhsshhooo sshhoo* as from deep below its massive body a whole cloud of steam blew. Slowly, as if reluctant to bid *adieu* to majestic Table Mountain, the train drew itself forward. Slowly. And, just as it gathered steam, Bhelekazi's father's face came up from one of the windows slowly pushing past: '*Sibali*,' the face said, '*Linye kuphel' itikit' endinalo!* Brother-in-law, I only have one ticket!'

'Men!' the condemnation, from the twelve, was unanimous. 'And to think he is so much older than she is,' said one voice I couldn't place.

'Well, that may be part of the problem.' That was Mother,

who continued, '… their dance steps may be out of sync.'

Another voice protested, and I knew that the speaker was Neo's mother. She had a throaty voice unlike any of the other mothers there. 'He is old, you say? But isn't he the one who left her, not the other way round?'

Here there was a lot of confusion, too many voices speaking all at once, each saying something different. I could not make out what exactly was being said. However, finally order was restored and a lone voice summed things up this way:

'It can happen that he left her to hide his shame. Perhaps, *uphelile*, he is finished.'

'So now, is he gone to his first wife?' My ears pricked at that. Golly! Then, Bhelekazi's mother was not her husband's first wife?

No sooner did that thought strike me than another, more sinister, came flooding my mind, chilling me to the bone.

Was Bhelekazi's mother her mother at all?

Once the one fact was challenged, to my way of thinking, all the other facts I knew about the family became suspect. Well, how did we know for sure that Bhelekazi was not, in fact, the child of the first wife?

The more I thought about this possibility, the more I liked it. To me, that made sense in several ways: It explained why her father took her away from the woman we thought was her mother. Of course, I reasoned, he was taking her to her rightful mother. Also, Bhelekazi's quietness was now explained, in my own mind, by her living with an impostor, a woman posing as her mother.

I had just about solved the whole mystery of Bhelekazi's family when Neo's mother shattered my theory.

'The brothers-in-law, it is said, want to skin him alive. They want their sister's daughter back!'

By and by, piece by piece, we figured out what was what and

who had done what to whom – to a certain extent, that is. A lot of questions remained unanswered, though. To this day, I have often wondered: Was Bhelekazi ever reunited with her mother? Whatever happened to that little, old-looking man, Bhelekazi's father? Did his brothers-in-law ever lay their hands on him?

Some weeks after Bhelekazi's family left our location, a man came to our door and asked, 'Where is Number Eleven?'

'I can't believe this! I can't believe this!' That is what he kept saying, over and over again, when we showed him the house next door to ours. But, finally, Father convinced him that, indeed, that incomplete-looking house was the house he sought.

'I will kill the rabid dog!' he'd vowed as he left.

The irate gentleman had paid a handsome sum of money to Bhelekazi's father for *icala lendlu*, which had been presented to him as '… a typical location house; just like all the others,' by that wily man.